I0822597

RAINBOW

BY THE SAME AUTHOR

Verse

Learning Not To Touch (Redbeck Press, 1998)
Reaching for a Stranger (Shoestring Press,1999)
Outstripping Gravity (Redbeck Press, 2000)
Exposures (Redbeck Press, 2003)
Taking Cover (Redbeck Press, 2005)
No Time for Roses (Salzburg Press, 2009)
Refuge (New Generation Publishing, 2012)

Narrative verse fantasy

Wish (Thames River Press, 2012)

www.michaeltolkien.com

...off came
the helmet to reveal piercing lively eyes
and golden hair thick and well groomed...

RAINBOW

A tale in verse by MICHAEL TOLKIEN

♦

After *The Other Side of the Rainbow* (1910),
a prose fantasy by Florence Bone

THAMES RIVER PRESS

Rainbow

THAMES RIVER PRESS
An imprint of Wimbledon Publishing Company Limited (WPC)
Another imprint of WPC is Anthem Press (www.anthempress.com)

First published in the United Kingdom in 2012 by

THAMES RIVER PRESS
75-76 Blackfriars Road
London SE1 8HA

www.thamesriverpress.com

A CIP record for this book is available from the British Library.

ISBN 978-0-85728-648-2

For Rosemary and everyone in our family

# Acknowledgements

The author would like to thank:

Rosemary, his wife, for reading every single more or less finished chapter draft and offering so much constructive and challenging advice.

Dorothy Jewitt, a remarkable authority on the life and work of Florence Bone, for her suggestion of *The Other Side of the Rainbow* as a work that might appeal to me.

Maureen Ward for reading this verse narrative with such empathy and insight, and for her meticulously prepared and executed illustrations, which provide further dimensions to the story.

Darin Jewell (Inspira Group Literary Agency) for his personal and professional support in securing the publication of this work.

Think Digital Print Ltd (Oakham) for their advice and production of initial copy.

Meadwell Ltd Artworks (Deeping St James) for scanning and processing of illustrations prior to publication.

Contents

Preface

Florence Bone's *The Other Side of the Rainbow* (1910), a now forgotten young children's fantasy, was my source for this verse narrative. I never thought of 'improving' on the original or making what I wrote dependent on knowing it. I was inspired to develop and adapt its implications and possibilities and write a tale with its own style, coherence and momentum. By coincidence, when I was about two-thirds of the way through writing *Rainbow* I saw the film based on *Alice's Adventures in Wonderland*, and it seemed to be conceived on similar principles in regard to Lewis Carroll's work. Two years ago though, wondering how to begin and rejecting every first chapter, I wrote in my notebook: *why alter and adapt this charming fantasy of innocence, colour and bizarre little capers? A century on I could read it comfortably to a child of 6, 7, or 8 years, so where do I come in?*

Its narrative outline is simple and the tale's unique flavour is derived less from its subject matter than from its lively, uncluttered and never sentimental characterisation of plants, creatures and larger-than-life figures, and from its internally consistent imaginative world presented in a gently humorous and coaxing style.

A little girl the author calls Plain Old-fashioned Jane, is chosen in infancy by benign 'fairy' figures to receive the gift of unaffected, open-minded wonder for and sympathy with the natural world, and to travel by unexpectedly roundabout ways to the mythical rainbow garden, bridge and palace as a means of developing and refining her responses. These lofty, ethereal places will provide the ultimate glimpses of perfection. But many of Jane's strangest and most challenging adventures arise from her willingness to assist Joyless Joe, who at first despises and distrusts all she has come to believe in and care for. Her way forward is sidetracked by a quest to acquire a silver spade, the means for this lad to make a new, exploratory start: she must visit an underground forge, a desert-dwelling giantess, and an under-hill nursery where all plants are cared for. Only then is she free to rise to higher realms of wonder but even here she is tested by her degree of concern for unfortunate figures, and just on the verge of the promised garden, forgetting warnings, finds her progress seriously threatened. After Jane reaches the heavenly palace the tale ends in a kind of romantic apotheosis. She is transformed into the ubiquitous maiden of post-Mallory quest-and-conquest yarns, and rides away with Sir Magic Wonderful. Earlier on this lonely, gallant, quasi-Arthurian knight has entertained her in his moonlit, gothic palace.

With some exceptions I have more or less followed Florence Bone's narrative scheme. Unlike Jane, my central character, Grace, is well into girlhood when she is tested with a choice of gifts. In addition to visiting '*The-Wood-That-Is-Not-There*' with its enhanced sense of nature's mysteriously benevolent power, my traveller has to pass through '*The-Wood-That-Must-Be-There*' where the retrospective contrasts and uninviting atmosphere present an unruly, tooth-and-claw post-Darwinian wilderness. My Rainbow Garden has many more contrasting scenes than in the source tale, and in my version the Rainbow Palace on the summit of the bow bridge is not the setting for the final scene. It is an enthralling place but one for finding perspectives and making choices about the future, whereas little Jane exits from here to dwell happily-ever-after with Sir Magic. In my tale he is Sir Substantial Nebule (or more familiarly Sir Cloudy Lost-Heart), an attractive figure but apparently caught in a time warp. Similar temptations to escape have been apparent at many stages of Grace's journey.

My final chapter is entitled 'Home?' (implying *where is it?* and *how is it reached?*) Grace descends the vanishing rainbow steps to meet again some of the principal characters she has encountered and make a choice of how best to go back and venture on in the world. Her return to the mundane moments when her journey began is meaningfully 'undramatic' but accompanied by a more vivid perception of detail.

I include all Florence Bone's characters: guiding 'fairy' figures of authority, birds, animals, plants, insects. But their appearance, disposition, behaviour and speech is often radically changed or developed to suit the purpose and concepts of my story. This also affects the content and style of the more lyrical passages attributed to them.

Without my realising it for some while, I adapted an appealing tale to write the kind of story of enchantment (a surprising but motivated journey into Faerie) along lines that might do justice to a genre which seems so often to have been misunderstood or abused.

The world entered into and journeyed through is not an escape, a dream or a holiday from reality but a series of places and encounters from which the adventurer discovers new perspectives about her own day-to-day experiences and the limitations these impose. The dreams twice provided by the Pan-like peddler are really gateways or transitions into new phases of Grace's quest. At the end she comments on how they lead 'to hard choices and anxious times.' Also her moving through the thin veils that divide the 'here and now' from the 'beyond' is not an end in itself; it prepares for a reinvigorated return. What she sees and hears does not set Grace apart from daily life but enables her to embrace it more positively. Certainly she experiences strange transformations, bold colours, unusual kinds of communication; but all are recognisable as derived from the living, evolving world as we know it, and physical obstacles and limitations remain as frustrating and confusing as ever. The figures, creatures and plants she meets are mostly wise and purposeful: there are no comfortably endearing or absurdly rapacious ornamental freaks who thrive in an aimless dream world. The inhabitants of 'Faerie', I feel, should be recognisable as living beings or things but with more dimensions, larger-than-life but not merely in the sense of physical appearance or potency.

Throughout I have avoided two debased and abused terms: 'fairy', either as noun or adjective, and 'magic'. The figures who advise and assist Grace are Guides and Guardians, and their *rôle*, partly mysterious, partly practical, and consistently beneficent, is global. Their wisdom is acquired, not artificially inherent, and they are one manifestation of universal forces at work in the earth's evolution. Their appearance in many forms is vital both to the story and to its implications. But it is primarily *about* Grace, not about them.

Why the focus on Grace, some may ask. Perhaps because the tale suggests that more is asked of those with talents and gifts, and they may be chosen to be tested by traversing wider realms that are both beyond and within. Here their elevating moments are only achieved by shouldering unexpected demands and adversities and by learning to see below and through surfaces. Grace is a child from a specific background but that does not mean the tale is only significant for children. She may be all or none of us, since one of its principal themes, indeed its *raison d'être*, is the retention and development of childlike wonder.

I have tried to give the 'extended' dimensions or fictional world that Grace enters consistency and coherence and a set of references protagonist and reader can accept and feel at home with. If what's called 'willing suspension of disbelief' needs to be made, the *spell* (in the ancient dual sense of story and imposed power) is broken. Once a fantasy tale becomes piecemeal and haphazard it loses conviction. Even so, both central figure and reader should also feel that many experiences cannot be easily explained away. Phenomena glimpsed in a world of peculiar, if within their context, 'believable' dimensions and occurrences, are no more likely to be fully understood than motives and contradictions of characters in 'conventional' fiction.

Michael Tolkien
31st January, 2011

Part 1

Chapters 1–6

ACROSS AND TOWARDS

A few quiet words about Grace

Grace was an orphan. When she was still a little, unchristened baby called Jane, her parents both died in a terrible accident. She had been adopted and brought up by an aunt and uncle. Aunt Miriam was her mother's much older sister. She and Uncle Edward had lost their baby and had had no more children. They called their niece Grace in thankfulness for the favour of her presence in their rather lonely life in a large, rambling three-storey house on the edge of a village. Its long gardens and orchards had grown wild where they met the open, well-wooded country. Uncle Edward would not give up his old family home and had to work longer and longer hours to provide for its upkeep. He was often away and abroad for weeks at a time. He was a shadowy, distant figure to Grace, quite kind and gentle but always too tired and worried to listen to what she wanted to tell him. Her aunt was just 'Mum', kind, loving and sometimes strict all in one, someone she wanted to please and tell everything that was on her mind without having to think if it mattered. Everything Grace had to say mattered to Mum.

Aunt Miriam read Grace many 'real-life' stories from all over the world, but she had no liking for what are often called '*fairy*' stories, as if to suggest that they are not 'true' and only for young children. She did however approve of and read aloud to her niece *Alice's Adventures in Wonderland* and *Through the Looking-Glass* because they made children realise there were no simple answers and that everything was something other than it seemed to be – and… well…wasn't the author so clever and witty! She also planned to read her niece many of the ancient legends. And Uncle Edward, when he had time, would talk about how things worked or what he thought would interest Grace about the natural world.

You may need to know this because unlike most children, apart from hearing a few stories at nursery school, Grace had no pictures or memories in her mind of the kinds of magical changes and shape-shifting you will see and hear with her. So she had never come across creatures out of nature talking with humans or having any thoughts like ours, or of something turning out to be quite different from what it seems to be. Radio, films, and television might have helped; but her story takes place before their time.

I

GIFT OF WONDER

A fairly long chapter in which Grace has a lot to learn.

Ask Grace about her first memories
and she'll be sure to say: lying awake early
on bright summer mornings while the trees touched
clouds and hid the sky behind their glossy coats.
Roses rambled up and around the open windows,
nodding to each other and keeping an eye on her.
She could hear bees up and about and busy
so long before her, buzzing into rose-hearts
to gather nectar for honey. Some settled a moment
on her window ledges. Had they stopped to wonder
who or what she was before going home
to their white hives beyond the long orchard?
Often a swallow perched on her lowered window.
Mister or Missus? She couldn't tell. It twittered, bowed
and flew up to its mud-hut nest under
the eaves, rough to look at, satin-smooth inside.
She knew they came to live here every summer, hatched
a family and took it overseas to warmer lands.

She didn't yet know that travelling far and wide
made these birds wiser than those who only lived
in one place. They knew that Grace was no
ordinary little girl, how thoughtful she was,
her delight in sights and sounds of summer mornings.
So they must soon tell the earth guardians
and guides who looked after plants, flowers and seeds
how at an early age she was content just to wonder.
Perhaps she'd be visited with gifts and advice.

So hidden and quiet are these beings that people like you
or me seldom notice them, and no one's sure
what shape or form they'll take. They only ever talk
to tell us something important, set a task or a test.
But swallows as they dip and swerve and swoop for bugs
can see them, know when to make them listen, or ask
favours in return for news from their travels.

✣ Gift of Wonder ✣

Best not to disturb them in broad daylight
when they watch over everything that grows
green, then dies down for a long rest
or to make way for something stronger and brighter.
Wait for dawns when the moon still shines
and their dancing and singing in open fields
or woodland glades is over, dances that might be
the rustle of birds through crisp leaves, songs
like a gentle wind shuffling through blades of grass.
For a moment they sit in circles to prepare
another day of clothing and adorning the earth.

Then they'll listen and talk and give advice which may
or may not be easy to understand at once.
And to the wise birds with their rose-dyed fronts,
sharp wings and forked tails they listened intently,
happy to hear about Grace and how, without knowing,
she delighted in the way they coloured and cared for
the living earth. Nine of their lively company
would visit her at sunrise when she lies awake,
watching and listening as the world comes alive.

As they glided through blossoming orchards and gardens
to the old, rambling house where Grace lived,
birds had begun their full early summer song.
Dew-laden leaves sparkled gold in dawn's
slanting light and the guardians breathed with delight
fresh scents from flowers they loved and tended.
It was like the unspoiled dawn of time we often
dream about but can't quite believe in, knowing
the wonders of planet Earth's long, slow unfolding.

Grace lay watching a low sun set light to
walnut and mulberry trees so they looked like
bouquets of green fire clutched by black fingers,
the long shadows of chimney stacks, when suddenly

she noticed an altogether brighter light blaze up
between her bed and windows. At first it seemed
to come from kindly faces, then from their tall
figures, each radiantly clothed in colours of flowers
she thought she recognised. She was not afraid,
just surprised, as if she'd opened a door into
a well-known room and found instead a lofty
conservatory lit up with flowering plants.
The first to speak was robed in petal-like folds
of purest white like the rose outside her window.
'We are flower guardians here to offer gifts.
We know our work delights you. Your choice will decide
the days ahead and colour your long life to come.'
(Was this a voice or a breeze among glossy leaves?)

How strange it was to lie there and feel important!
But Grace felt she had to look and listen with care
while the guardians showed and explained their gifts,
though all the details you will hear about seemed
to take no time at all, so quickly and quietly spoken
were they, their movements graceful as shapes and shadows
of plants and flowers their garments made her think about.
First Carnation Red unveiled from nowhere
a spray of flowers whose shape and colour never stayed the same.
'This gift will make you the best of gardeners.'
Then Marigold Amber held out a purse
edged with silver, fastened by golden studs, embroidered
in multi-coloured silks. 'Open this to become rich,
build upon your riches, be envied and admired.'
But Sunflower Yellow outshone her sister, dazzling Grace
with a mirror framed in finely-crafted wood and gems.
'With my gift you will be sure of yourself,
amaze the world with discoveries and travels.'

Camomile Green seemed more kind and loving.
She unwrapped a shawl that looked like a field

of waving daisies. 'Take this gift to put others
first and wrap them warmly in your care.' Her close
companion, Deep-Pink Clover, watched and smiled
but had no gift to give except her perfect scent,
while Forget-Me-Not Blue showed Grace a book,
its leather spine hinged in turquoise jewels,
its covers front and back flecked with sapphire.
'Open this and you will hear every sound
whatever its pitch, and speak so well everyone
will listen to your words and praise your powerful voice.'
Darker blue than her was wood-shaded Bell,
who drew a tiny casket from her nightfall robe.
'This changes colour as your thoughts turn over.
Look inside and see deeper and further than ever.

Six tempting gifts! Should Grace choose now?
No. Another figure was coming towards her.

Purple Heartsease seemed to offer a bunch
of sturdy little field pansies, but they folded
into a smooth stone with smoky shades of violet.
'When you feel wonder, roll this amethyst
gently between your left palm and fingers
and you will see silken threads of purply-white
entering your stone. It will grow close to you
as time goes by, and in it you'll begin to find
strange scenes or faces that have much to say.'

All at once without knowing why, Grace
reached out and took this stone, no bigger
than her slender thumb, light as tissue paper.
Her test was over, and the guardians looked pleased
as they faded from sight so that even a perfect
summer morning seemed a little less bright.
But Heartsease stayed and sat on the bed beside her.
'Why were there all those wonderful choices?

None seemed right, then I took your gift
which I don't think I really understand.'
'What you will begin to see,' answered Heartsease,
'is that all those other blessings work less well
if you lack the gift of open-minded wonder.
Achievements and adventures should surprise or sadden,
make your heart leap or shrink, teach you to think.'
'Suppose I give up wondering? What then?' asked Grace.
'You will grow old before your time.' 'Surely old
people still wonder,' insisted the little girl.

'Think of it like this,' replied Heartsease firmly.
'People who wonder never grow old. Their hair
may be white, their skin cracked and legs weak
but the gift of wonder keeps them young and alert.
Like yours their hearts and minds can discover
what lies within and beyond the Rainbow.
And you are just beginning a long journey that will
unravel this mystery as long as you follow
your stone and fill it with feelings of wonder.'
'Rainbows shine and vanish. They're a trick of light,
my uncle tells me,' said Grace. 'Looked at one way
that's true,' replied Heartsease, smiling kindly.
'But wonder shows you more than meets the eye.
Even we guardians appeared like a rainbow.
Remember the colours? If you are patient
your wonder stone can lead you to the rainbow
and beyond, revealing that every answer
is only the start of many more questions.

Grace, whose aunt and uncle always liked her
to ask questions and tried to answer them,
was excited but puzzled by these strange ideas.
'How can *I* do all this *and* discover
everything you've told me about?' Heartsease
only laughed gently and said: 'It's now time

for me to go about my work among my flowers.
Think of purples, mauves and violets and think of all
I've said. Keep wondering about what you see
and hear, and fill your precious stone with these thoughts.
Watch its colours and patterns grow richer
and more intricate. Don't hide your gift.
No one will ever be able to see or touch it.
Your adventure has just begun. We'll soon meet
to start its funny, sometimes fearful journey.'
And even as she spoke the lovely guardian became
part of morning light and summer colours
that seemed to dance and summon Grace outside.

✤ Rainbow ✤

We are flower guardians here to offer gifts.
We know our work delights you. Your choice will decide
the days ahead and colour your long life to come…

She must have been daydreaming. It was still early.
No one was moving about the house. Had any
time passed at all? But she was still clutching
the polished amethyst in her left hand.
What could she say to Aunt Miriam? Uncle
would laugh before she had finished. No words
could describe what she had learned and felt.
Perhaps she sensed that words can break a spell
and wonder can't be shared with someone else.

II

DREAM PEDLAR

✵

A chapter in which Grace finds out how she has to put up with being puzzled.

Not many weeks later Grace wandered beyond
the crumbling walls of formal flower gardens
to see how well the orchard trees were showing
their first tiny fruits, and feed scraps to the geese
her uncle kept there to peck the grass down.
As they squabbled and screeched over their food,
Grace glanced at her amethyst and found it
pale and patchy, as if waiting for new colours.
Then she thought she heard a voice singing nearby.
Was it coming from a bush, a tree or from beyond
the tall thorn hedges? Struck by its piercing
sweetness she began to rub her stone between
her palm and fingers and to hear these words:
Among violets below the hedge
I'm waiting for you.
Heartsease always keeps her pledge.
She's here to guide you.
The stone was ablaze with dancing purple flames.

'Violets are so small and frail, how could
they conceal the tall, graceful Heartease?'
asked Grace, as she searched the shaded hedgerow.
And just as she was about to give up altogether
the guardian came smiling towards her in long folds
of airy, shimmering violet. Like a long-lost friend
she drew Grace into a close embrace that smelt
of delicate scents, fresh leaves and warm earth.
How could she be so warm and loving and yet
so quick to fade or shrink beyond sight and touch?
'I'm no nearer to finding the way to the Rainbow
and beyond, as you described it. Can you
help me now?' To which Heartsease replied,

singing in the voice that had filled the orchard:
It's up and down a staircase,
Through and beyond a wood.
Just follow where dreams lead,
And do whatever you should.

'But I want to start at once,' argued Grace.
'You should be eager but not in a hurry,'
answered the guardian firmly. 'It's not a race!
And if you're in a rush you won't stop to fill
your stone and make it more precious with the riches
of wonder. Dwell on every surprise or you will never
reach your goal.' 'First please tell me the way.'
But with a wave of her hand Heartsease seemed
all at once to say goodbye, bless the girl with luck,
and sweep herself away into thin air.
And though the day was warm and still, Grace noticed
how a breeze combed and shook the clumps of violets,
which somehow made her feel even more alone
in her quest for the Rainbow and its mysteries.
Why not begin by following the long, white
dusty lane that ran beside this tall, dense hedge?
Long ago she'd found a way to squeeze underneath
where rabbit burrows had undermined the roots.

After crawling over loose earth Grace scrambled
through nettles, hedge parsley and giant hogweed
and across a sodden ditch onto the rutted lane:
where were the carts, horsemen, other passers-by?
On the other side as far as she could see each way
ran a high wall of yellow stone and over it hung
here and there branches of ash and elm, dragged
down by clinging ivy. Along one there ran
a red squirrel. It paused to look down at her,
tail still waving from its headlong rush.
Did it just blink or was it winking at her?

No use talking to animals, but so many
strange things had happened, why not try?
'Please, does this lane lead to the Rainbow?'
It looked alert and pointed a foreleg at the ditch.
There, oddly clear among green surroundings, sat
a fat emerald frog. Its wide-open mouth
made it look too content to notice Grace.

It hopped towards her as if it knew she'd something
to say. Stooping down she asked respectfully:
'Can you tell me the way to the Rainbow?'
Frogs are not polite. 'Ask the Owl,' it croaked,
and jerked its broad head towards a thick cluster
of ivy hanging from the wall. Grace felt
she was being tossed rudely back and forth
across the lane. And then she saw two eyes
watching her through a screen of ivy leaves.
Their heavy lids blinked and creased in a way
that made them look worldly-wise and full of knowledge.
Surely the owl would think her foolish. She must
be patient if he spoke. It felt like a 'he'.

...she saw two eyes
watching her through a screen of ivy leaves
their heavy lids blinked and creased in a way
that made them look worldly-wise and full of knowledge.

His voice seemed to come from deep in his chin
and must have been muffled in thick feathers.
'I have no idea, none at all,' he muttered,
As if to say 'how should *I* know?' and 'why
am *I* being bothered with questions *I* can't answer?'

Which left Grace feeling foolish and bad-tempered.
But a friend she'd never met happened to fly
overhead: the swallow who once told the guardians
she had the gift of wonder. He swooped down,
zigzagged about her and said in a breathless
twitter: 'Ask flowers that colour and cheer the verges
of the lane. They won't just pretend to help.'
Was this another hoax, she wondered. She passed
red campions that looked puffed up and proud,
feathery stitchwort that bent away and wanted to
be left alone, but a cluster of speedwells caught
her attention, and as she stopped to admire
their sea-blue petals they seemed to return her gaze
and asked in a welcoming chorus: *Can we help*?
'Thank you. I doubted if I should ask,' said Grace,
outspoken as ever. 'You are so frail, wither
so soon and only live here.' The answer was
a chime of finely-tuned bells. They were laughing!

It's not like you who have the gift of wonder
to think we're ornaments that fade away.
The way we live and die and live and die
is slow but sure, and makes us all the stronger.

The more folk hurry, the less time have they
for things that grow and creep and spread.
Look and listen in unlikely corners. Fill
your precious stone with thoughts of us.

Stooping closer, Grace found each flower
had its own face, a delight she wound into
her wonder stone, and asked: 'Don't you die?'

We feel weary so our petals flop and fade
making way for seeds to grow and spread.
Our colour's stored by careful guardians.
One day you'll visit Nature's Nursery
and see that nothing's lost or wasted.
Everything returns and helps to make
this living world you love and wonder at.

You are on the right road for the Rainbow,
through The-Wood-That-Is-Not-There,
visiting the Halls of Guardian Spirits.
The Dream Pedlar will guide you.

So much to grasp whenever she dealt with flowers!
Grace felt lost. 'Where is this pedlar of dreams?'
Where the long white lane turns north
he'll be waiting if you're in luck.
Maybe we'll meet again. Who knows?

As she thanked them and at last made her way
along the lane, a voice like the one she heard
in the orchard filled the air with piercing song.

Who knows the secret tint of speedwell blue
Or why forget-me-nots are seldom blue?

Who can teach us what the thrushes have to say,
Or why the lark sings best at break of day?

Who can smell the wild rose scent, or tell
Us how its heart-shaped petals work their spell?

Where the lane turned, a weathered stile parted
the hedge. And under its tent of dog rose
sat the Pedlar of Dreams. Not a road-weary,
ageing pedlar like those who called at home
with heavy packs of sewing things or gaudy trinkets
laid out in rows and curves to tempt your purse.
This young wanderer was cleanly dressed
in beech-leaf green, his dark, curly hair threaded
with ferns. One small satchel lay beside him.
He was fitting together a long, silver pipe,
and when he played Grace began to twist and turn
as if the notes were urging her to sing and dance.
But she was not the only one to feel like this.
At the piper's feet stretched velvet moss, surely
a carpet to display his pack of dreams?... No!
Summoned by his pipe and swaying to its spell,
tiny creatures from field and hedge were gathering there,
meeting for the strangest dance you could imagine.

Beetles with green and silver wings danced beside
tortoiseshell butterflies. Two lines
of ladybirds faced each other like soldiers
in red and black, moving together and stepping back
in perfect time and order. Two centipedes
lounged in the sun. Why dance? Their days
were filled with scuttling here and there. A bumble bee
danced with a dragon fly until they grew tired.
The bee made for the shade of a white dead-nettle
while the vain dragonfly spread her glassy wings
that shimmered like mother of pearl when sunlight
touched them, as she made sure it did,
impressing the bee who brought her a drink
in an acorn cup, and fanned her with a feather

twice its size. 'Don't!' she snapped. 'You'll blow me
off my feet.' And the feather danced away with the cup.
Grace clapped with delight and wonder at
the way everything danced when this pedlar piped.

Even some nearby branches of oak rose and fell
while Grace danced and wove the wonder of it all
into her purple stone until it shone. Then suddenly
the piping stopped in the middle of a tune,
everything went still, the moss had vanished
and all the smart little insects with it. 'Now, Grace,'
said the pedlar softly, 'after the fun and dancing
you'd maybe like to rest and try one of my dreams.'
'Yes I would,' she said, 'but first please show me
the way to The Rainbow.' 'You'll learn that
in your dream. It's not the sort you have in bed.
It's a waking dream, a new kind of seeing
that will guide you to *The-Wood-That-Is-Not-There*.
Rest in the long, dry grass while I find the best
one for you.' And taking out a shorter, broader
ebony pipe, he played a slow, soothing melody.
Soon Grace felt her eyes grow heavy and dim,
and nearby buttercups turned to golden mist.

…under a tent of dog rose
sat the Pedlar of Dreams. Not a road-weary,
ageing pedlar like those who call at home…

III

RAINBOW BRIDGE

A chapter where Grace finds that a dream is not a way out of problems and that help arrives in unexpected ways.

Grace felt as if she'd woken up still deep
in the dream provided by the green pedlar,
walking just before sunrise steeply down
a narrow cobbled street crowded with wooden buildings,
all shapes and sizes. A deserted old town
like the ones she'd seen in picture histories
that Aunt Miriam said were made up by the artist.
Nothing showed that anyone had lived here,
no scuttling rats, no stray cats or dogs,
not one sparrow chattering under the eaves.
All she could hear was the echo of her footsteps,
and turning a corner that seemed far below the place
she'd started from, Grace was amazed to see
broad meadows full of rushes and ancient willows
that ended in a deep, slow-moving river,
so fearfully wide that trees on the far side looked
like bushes, and she wondered if anything else
grew or moved in the haze beyond this leaden sheet.

There were no wharfs or boats tied up and none
of the webfoot birds Grace loved to watch dive,
feed and quarrel. She felt small, lonely
and ignored by this murky monster as its body
slid endlessly past without a splash or ripple.
Thick mist began to veil the landscape beyond;
but as the sun was about to rise, the sky above
was lined with every colour like a rainbow lying
sideways, which made her spirits rise: 'at least
I'm facing the right way!' she shouted, throwing
her gemstone into the air. Back in her palm
it felt heavier and was striped like the horizon
but in endless varieties of mauve and purple,
as if to tell her the way ahead was clearer.
Which was all very well: 'but there's no bridge,
no boat, and I don't have wings, though people

in dreams are supposed to float over obstacles.'
Should she turn back and find some other way?

Then came the first sound since she had woken
in this empty place. It began like a mixed
tinkle and whisper approaching through the grass.
Slowly she began to trace the pedlar's sleepy tune
that soon changed to a brisk march played on
the silver pipe, and along with it the rustle
of countless little feet, which became a bright
procession of insects coming to greet her.
First nine brimstone-yellow butterflies
showing off their fine red-dotted wings.
Grace thought they led the way to add colour
rather than because they were of any use!
There followed twelve serious-looking beetles
with shiny green backs. They reminded her
of pompous councillors parading towards
a town hall. And after them stalked long-legged
spiders, each wearing coloured numbers from one
to twenty-four, perhaps to show they meant business!

They trod neatly as if dancing to the pedlar's pipe
in front of nine prosperous-looking black and yellow
bumble bees, walking in three ranks of three,
dusted with yellow pollen, a sign of hard work.
Now as the company circled her, Grace, who liked
to play with numbers, counted fifty-four in all,
then found that all the digits of each little group
totalled half that sum. What could *that* mean?
But since they had drawn up round her and seemed
to be waiting for something, she asked: 'Who are you?
Where have you come from? Can you do anything
to help me over this deep, impassable river?'
Each group sang to her, and Grace listened
patiently, quite used to misleading answers.

Strong webs strung across
Will weave the frame we need
To throw a bridge across
And serve you in your need, sang the spiders.

Paved with beetle backs
Often shed but never lost,
Your path will show no cracks
Tarmac-tight without the cost! sang the beetles.

We'll glue up spindly spider nets
Just in case they fray,
And seal the plated way.
You'll see how well our honey sets, sang the bees.

We'll flutter high into rainbow sky,
Floating back with strongest strands
About and about to weave and tie.
The brighter the bridge the firmer it stands, sang the butterflies.

Strange and rather jingly plans, and each group
insisted on singing at once to a different tune,
though Grace was glad they'd come to help.
And several spiders started by throwing their fine silk
lines over the river, looking as if they trod on air
while they scurried across to fix them on the far bank.

Once these pioneers returned, all twenty-four
began to spin vast gossamer webs above
this great stretch of moving water, weaving in
and out, round and round until it hung and swayed,
elastic but strong, like a see-through suspension bridge.
Then some beetles brought the promised backplates
from a secret store, while others laid and overlapped them
along the tight webs to make a shiny track
that ran dazzlingly straight into the sun's path:
slippery till the bees dusted it with pollen
before they checked for loose webs or plates and stuck them
down with honey that smelt sweet but gripped like steel.
Though it was not yet safe for Grace to cross.
Butterflies flew into the rainbow-tinted dawn
Till their tiny beating wings vanished.
Soon they returned with long coloured plaits,
and all the workers helped to swathe and bind up
the spider structure till it became a floating rainbow.

Grace was sorry she'd thought butterflies only
for show. They'd used the power of light to weld
the work together. 'I won't forget your soaring flight
and I'll never think of you as ornaments.'
'Well! Well!' exclaimed a leading spider, 'Praise
always goes to good looks and star performance!'
'I'd not forgotten you, not one of you,'
protested Grace. 'I watched with wonder as you spun
those seven and twenty webs – yes: I did count! –
across your long, strong lines and made them arches
to carry the plated way. You will walk beside me.
The others will follow to show respect for what you've done.'

Grace began to see that those who'd helped her along
this journey liked a kind word. And stepping off
the strong and gently swaying bridge on the far side
she turned round to thank the bees and beetles.

Her friends had vanished and their rainbow bridge
was no more than a few fading coloured plumes.

IV

DOWNCAST DON

✵

A chapter in which Grace meets someone unhappy and gives a promise which will make her journey more complicated than she could ever have realised.

The shock brought her 'down to earth', a place
Aunt Miriam said was better than 'head in the clouds'.
'Have I really praised insects and argued with them?
Did they help me over that Mississippi of a river?'
The water was real enough, still going about
its sluggish business through the sunny landscape,
ignoring Grace who felt very much alone.
But imagine her surprise when she turned
again to look at what had seemed from afar
a hazy wilderness, and saw great white
gates with tall, fat posts and countless bars
thicker than her wrists. The wonder of it
made her rub the amethyst into a rich
violet full of secrets and mystery.
Somehow she knew she must find a way
beyond; but how could she move anything
so heavy and with such massive locks and hinges ?
Even if she had a key, could she turn it?

Looking through the painted bars she realised
this gateway led into a widespread forest,
not dark but glowing with a green light
that came from its many winding grassy paths
and millions of ferns along them. These seemed
to beckon her as they bent to the breeze.
Tall foxgloves, white, purple and deep mauve
also nodded in welcome. And in the shaded grass
thousands of insects crawled and danced as if
they knew that Grace was watching. Stranger still,
she began to hear faint music high above her.
Perhaps the wind piped and hummed a tune that came
and went as it blew and caught its breath.
But none of this would open the gates. And across
their curved top bars were inscribed these words:
The-Wood-That-Is-Not-There: that place

the speedwells and Dream Pedlar had said
she *must* visit to fulfil her rainbow journey.

A trick of sunlight showed Grace a brass key
hanging on a burnished hook high up
one of the round posts, well beyond her reach.
If she were lucky like Alice in Wonderland
she might find magic liquid to make her grow.
As it was she only just stopped herself
from sitting down in despair, but then she looked at
her stone, turning it over as if to ask its advice.
For answer it slipped away into the long grass
and landed – can you believe it? – beside a boy
lying fast asleep in the wood-edge shadows.
He was about her age but a lot taller.
Perhaps he could reach the key, thought Grace, and knelt
gently down to wake him. But he needed shaking!
'What's the matter? I'm not ready to wake up,'
he grumbled, his sleep-caked eyes tightly shut.
'But it's morning and I need your help now.
A pedlar and flowers and insects have helped me, won't you?

I'm on my way to find out what lies within
and beyond the rainbow. So would you try
to reach that key up there and we can walk along
green paths in the wonderful wood that lies beyond?'
All he'd heard so far was the word 'key'.
'What key? You must be seeing things!' 'Look!
It's up on that gate post.' Grace longed for
some lively flowers or insects with brains and eyes.
But at least the boy leapt up and stared hard. 'I see
no key and no gate. What *are* you *on* about?'
'It's the gate into that wood,' insisted Grace.
And he looked even more blank. 'Wood?
For miles around there's nothing but windswept bushes.'
Now it was her turn to stare in disbelief.
Might as well ask him his name, she thought.
'I'm Donald, changed by grown-ups to Downcast Don,
Don-in-the-Dumps or just *Down*-in-the-Dumps.
The few friends I've got call me Doncast or Downer.

Grace wondered whether to laugh or feel sorry.
'Your nicknames make you sound unhappy,' she said.
Perhaps this was why he saw a dull heath
strewn with bushes and not the lively green wood.
'So what's your name?' asked Downcast Don as if
he didn't care and seldom wondered about anything.
'Grace,' she said proudly. 'Not a proper name,'
said Don with a gurgle that might have been laughter.
'Think what you like. I'm happy with it,'
she said and threw her stone high into the air.
But coming down it slipped past her open palm
and rolled away until it rested under the gate.
Which Grace took to mean that she ought to look
into the wood, and wonder about seeing it
while Don could not. 'What's that?' he asked
when she picked up the amethyst. 'You're always

tinkering with it. Looks like a glass bead.'
'This gemstone is worth more than any jeweller's price.

Filled with my thoughts, when I feel wonder
it's become part of me, and guides me in strange,
unexpected ways, not always easy to follow,
though they all bring me nearer to the rainbow.'
'Who filled your head with this? It sounds like
nonsense to me.' The boy seemed bored and yawned loudly.
'Heartsease, the flower guardian, gave me the stone,
taught me its powers and how to respect them.'
Don laughed though it sounded like painful choking.
'You're living in dreamland. Grow up and discover
the real world. The only flower guardians I know
are gardeners, and what do they know about gems?'
He looked at Grace as if she were half his size.
Aunt and Uncle would have agreed but their advice
was given kindly. And she surprised herself into
wanting to behave like them. Without a thought
she held out her precious stone. 'Just borrow it:
you'll see much more than you thought was there.'

He shrugged his shoulders as if to say: 'Why bother?'
But he took it in his weather-beaten hand,
and faced the way Grace said there was a gate
and a wood, rather like a lost rambler
who can't believe what his compass tells him.
Then a smile dawned over Don's sullen face,
his eyes opened wide for the first time
since Grace had woken him, dark brown and kindlier
than she supposed, and he was not weighed down
like someone grown old before his time. He reached
for the key, and looking her straight in the eye said:
'I see what you mean: the plants and insects feel
alive as if they are waiting to be noticed.
Here's the key. You should get into that

interesting world and turn your back on
these flat marshy lands that never seem to end.'
'Won't you join me?' she asked, fitting the key.
Giving her back the stone he looked almost tearful:

'I'd be lost with nothing to guide me like your jewel.'
'Perhaps Heartsease will provide you with something
like this gift if I meet her. She often arrives
when least expected. And then you will find your way
to the Rainbow and its many mysteries.'
'Don't forget to mention me,' begged Don, as Grace
turned the key and the gates opened without a murmur.
Looking round she couldn't see him but shouted:
'I wont forget!' and rubbed this pledge into her stone.

V

THE-WOOD-THAT-IS-NOT-THERE

⁂

Where Grace finds that everything and everyone is very much there, alive and alert and with a lot to say that does not help much with her new task.

At last Grace was in the place she must visit
to find her way to the rainbow and discover
its mysteries. And she was at once amazed
by how much rich and varied grass carpeted
the forest floor, even in deep and damp shade.
Each blade seemed to have its own green,
and each could be a person of any age dressed
in tight robes fastened by sapphire buckles;
or were these lingering dew drops that sparkled
in the wavering sunlight? Leaves of tallest trees
swayed above her head in a dance of welcome
but when she looked again they were quite still.
Grace thought she heard the words of Heartsease:
Wonder shows you more than meets the eye.
Was she learning to savour what she thought she saw?

Of course many might pass through this wood
and find it no different from any other wood
or, like Don, not even know it's a wood.

Everything that grew or moved was so busy.
Insects that crawled, flew, hummed or buzzed
seemed to invite her to take part in making
this shaded world the lively place it was,
as if awareness and wonder were not enough.
Her stone was all zig-zags, every kind
of mauve and purple weaving and twisting together.
She trod softly and quietly so as not to disturb
or crush something with its own mind or feelings.
Moving this way sharpened her senses so much
she soon felt tired and longed to sit and rest.
And that was when she found a green-mantled pool
below mossy banks, open to sky and sunlight.
The water was there before her but she felt
it was not really in the wood or part of it,
and all the woodland sounds echoed round,

like distant music that rises and fades in the wind;
but where better to sit and ease her aching legs?

Perched on an overhanging bough of pale alder
a dark brown song thrush piped some shrill phrases
and paused to look down at Grace. 'I'll sing
you to sleep if you like.' She closed her eyes
but then she seemed to see Downcast Don
looking lost, and remembered how she'd promised
to help him receive a gift of wonder like hers.
Ways of doing such kindness should be found
somewhere in this wood. She must be on her way.
'My song!' snapped the thrush. 'Not good enough
for you, I suppose!' 'I like every note,'
said Grace politely. 'But I'm worried about a boy
left outside the wood because he can't see it.
Please can you help me to find him a gift
like this?' She held up her glittering amethyst.
The thrush ruffled his feathers and hardly turned his head.
'No, I can't! People mostly walk here alone.
Now and again I see two who love each other.'

...the lily happened to catch his eye
and birds like to be ready with a quick answer.
'She's very proud but might be able to tell you.'

'Ah well,' sighed Grace. 'I can't say I love
Downcast Don that much, but I'd still like him
to see and explore the wood. He's all alone.'
'Ask Water Lily.' The thrush tilted his head
to look wise. The lily happened to catch his eye,
and birds like to be ready with a quick answer.
'She's very proud but might be able to tell you.'
The lily floated so close below the bank
Grace had not seen her white and gold splendour.

And even if she'd heard all this, the idle plant
took no notice. The thrush was right about her pride.
She spent every day admiring herself in the water.
Leaning over the edge of the pond Grace said:
'Water Lily, how can a poor, ragged boy
like Downcast Don enter the wood with no gift
to guide him?' The dazzling flower shuddered
and seemed to speak to herself as she floated off,
pushing aside pond mantel to show her disgust.

'No! no! Don't bring him in here,'
she muttered. 'I'd grow pale and horribly faint
at the sight of him. The very idea disturbs me.'
At least the thrush had greeted her and tried
to help, even if he was touchy and stuck-up,
but the lily, like the pond she lived in, somehow
did not fit into *The-Wood-That-Is-Not-There*
that welcomes and befriends everyone who finds
a way in: something Grace sensed but wasn't yet
sure about. So once again she felt lost
and confused. Even her stone had lost its lustre.
But just then there flashed down into the clearing
two sharp-edged black wings that flickered round
and dipped over the pool. It was the swallow
who'd saved her from unhelpful advice once before.
In too much of a hurry to stop he circled

her head and whispered as quickly as he flew:
'Woodmaster!…age-old…always tries to help…'

'Where is he?' shouted Grace. For answer the swallow
darted at a dark arch below tall trees
then shot up and away over their crests.
She ran out of broad daylight and plunged into
a deeply green, dimly lit cavern of trunks and branches.
Its floor was thick with leaves and smelt strongly
of brightly-coloured fungi, all shapes and sizes.
She felt a large, quiet being was there. It waited
to see if she was the sort of visitor to notice.

Unless she was mistaken, it had no feet,
was wrapped in a long grey-green, furrowed coat
criss-crossed with swathes of ivy. Its long arms
opened out into branches instead of fingers.
It seemed to shelter below an umbrella of oak leaves
under which two dark brown eyes that shone
with slowly-earned knowledge looked at her
as if she were expected, and a long branch-finger
invited her to come closer, and be listened to.

You may wonder why Grace was not afraid.
It must have been the calm, the feeling that
all rush and fuss was left behind outside the wood
whose most ancient tree was this great oak.
Many who passed that way would only see it
as a sturdy old survivor, but Grace asked:
'Are you the Woodmaster?' 'Some call me that.'
(She thought he sounded like a mixture of warm rumble
and crisp rustle.) 'I am also called other names:
Slow-Oak, Woodwise, Oakmaster, Shadewatcher…
I won't go on! I've lost count of the centuries
since I sprang from an acorn. My spirit
stretches back far beyond, so long has it chosen

to dwell in the changing dress of tree after tree.'
'So you can surely tell me how to find a wonder gift
for a lost friend,' said Grace hopefully.
'I only look one way and cannot tell you
about things or places I have never seen.
Some think me stupid and set in my ways.'
The old oak sighed and shook its heavy load of leaves.
'I don't think so,' said Grace. 'I do thank you
for that,' he replied. 'Compliments are so rare!'
But before she lost hope Grace felt something
brush to and fro at the hem of her long dress.
A single bluebell who had managed to flower
in this dim light wanted her to stop and listen.
'Woodmaster looks too high and sees little.

But I can tell you where to find Heartsease.'
The very name encouraged her: 'She's the one
who can give me a gift to help Downcast Don.'
'Don't be too sure,' warned Blue Bell.
'He may be too old or lost to be helped.
The guardian knows best. She spends summer
nights in a cavern below the wood's stoutest
wych elm. It spreads its pliant branches widely
in that lighter, airier place ahead of you.

Pass under the green elm tent and look for a door
that opens on a hall below the trunk and roots.
At sunset, knock and Heartsease will invite you in.'
It seemed a long while but the wood slowed up
everything to make you wait and watch.
Had she not done so she might have missed
this uneven little song that helped time pass.
It sounded very much like a soft breeze
shuffling through meadows tall with grass and herbs.

✣ Rainbow ✣

We're living spears,
every shade of green,
that spring and wither and spring again.

We watched you pass
and pause to find us gathered under trees.
Clever you were to spot us
as we seemed to come and go in the breeze.

We're tightly wrapped
in every kind of green.
We're the swaying troops you think you've seen.

The jewels we wear are buckles of the dew
that burns away,
returns each day
and makes us seem so perfectly clean and new.

There's nothing we miss.
So sit and listen to us
and find the best way how,
whatever you need to know.

VI

HEARTSEASE AT HOME

✵

Some questions and answers that make Grace realise that keeping her promise will need some strange travels that seem unlikely to lead her to the rainbow.

As shadows lengthened Grace noticed the elm door
she couldn't have seen without her wonder stone.
But while it danced in swirls to match the lively song
there was time to think about this strange wood.
What had it to do with her rainbow quest?
What would Aunt Miriam say about a place
free from danger where no one knew or did that much.
She'd no time for never-never lands and yet
the long search to help poor Don would please her,
and at least her niece was learning not to be too sure
that people and things were what they looked and sounded like.
And then Grace saw the reddening sun sink down
behind cloud turrets of rose and mauve and grey.
The wood lost its deep golden evening light
and began to look like a sketch in pen and ink.
Time to knock. The tree trunk door seemed to
fling itself aside, or was it opened by a line of ladybirds
that greeted her like servants in special uniform?

Some wore red coats, some yellow but all had
their own patterns or numbers of black spots or splashes.
Grace thought Heartsease must trust them with many tasks,
but wondered how she, a grown girl, could enter
a tree by this door and walk freely down
the long passage led politely by ladybirds
larger and smarter than she'd ever seen before.
The guardian had so far seemed larger than life
but as the descending hall became a wide room
there she was in a violet gown quietly stirring
an iron pan that stood on hewn stones over
glowing logs. She looked up to welcome Grace
as if she were expected, calling a ladybird
to keep an eye on the simmering mixture.
As she invited her to sit on simply-carved
log chairs in this warm underground kitchen,

furnished mostly with what the wood provided,
Heartsease was homely in the way she moved and spoke.

If only I could spend the night here, thought Grace,
knowing she must ask how to help Downcast Don,
which might well mean setting out in the dark.
'Have you enjoyed your travels so far?' asked the guardian.
Your stone has gathered many shades and patterns.
It shows you've begun to wonder about much
that is overlooked in this surprising world.'
'I've learned to watch and listen more closely,
and to wait. But I need to ask you at once
if you know of Don whose life's so dull and empty.'
'I do,' said Heartsease. 'But he won't know me.
He can't see beyond or behind what meets the eye.'
'He's changed and wants to learn,' insisted Grace.
'I gave him my precious gift for a moment.
He saw the gate and wood beyond, noticed
its busy growth and life and felt them calling him.
Surely he deserves the chance of a gift like mine.'
Her guide and loving friend was moved and pleased.

'Don cannot be given a wonder jewel like yours,
He's grown too old in his dull, blinkered ways.'
'So he will never enter the wood,' said Grace,
tearfully disappointed after her long wait.
'He can if he receives a spade cunningly forged
in well-tempered steel to look like polished silver.
You must provide it for him but also find and ask
the Mother of All Guardians to show him how
to use it and make his digging useful and curious.

Then he'll learn that all is not as it seems
and there's much to discover and wonder about.
This will start him on his own path to the Rainbow
and all it has to say to everyone who finds it.

But the task will be long and difficult for you
and it must be undertaken gladly and with courage.
Believe me, it helps to pave your own hard road
that reaches the Rainbow by many twists and turns.'

A great deal for Grace (and us) to think about.

Just then the ladybird told to watch the pan
said: 'the mixture's boiling and turning dark and frothy.'
Following the guardian to the hearth Grace asked
what was being prepared. It didn't smell like food.
'I'm testing out colours for plants I attend to.
Not for show. Every shade and tone must suit
where they grow, guiding in bees whose patient search
for nectar helps turn flower heads to seeds.
Colour makes my families live year after year.

Now it's time to think about helping Don.
You'll have to be lowered down a well shaft
and look for a forge deep under ground.
Its Mighty Smith is past-master of his craft.
His work is finely-made, useful and long-lasting.
He's not a giant as some call him, just so powerful
that when he laughs, or curses his one-eyed helpers,
the ground far above trembles for miles around.
He likes to live among rocks that hide the ore
mined and smelted into iron he hammers and shapes.
Heaps of dead wood from forests above burn
in his fires blown by bellows to white heat.
Their smoke and steam rise through twisting pipes
and smother nearby marshland like morning mist.'

Grace knew village blacksmiths who said little
and worked hard but always smiled or winked at her
as they bent or shaped red worms of hot iron
that hissed and sizzled in the black cooling trough.

What if such strength were cruelly used, she wondered.
Would this smith of caverns and tunnels listen
and agree to make the silver spade she needed?
And before that there was the well. 'Simple!'
said Heartsease, as if she'd heard Grace think.
'Remember the green folk who sang to you
by the elm. They'll lower and guide you safely
to the passages and workrooms. Now rest until
dawn when I'll guide you to the well top.'

The guardian thought it wise not to tell her
they'd pass through *The-Wood-That-Must-Be-There*,
ragged and unfriendly, quite unlike the one above them,
and best encountered with no time to think about it.
But now ladybird attendants brought a meal
of honey, fruit, seeds and spring water, and Grace
lay on a bed of dried, flower-scented leaves,
the amethyst on her forehead until she fell asleep,
to clear and calm her thoughts for a fresh start.

Part 2

Chapters 7–12

OVER AND UNDER

VII

THE-WOOD-THAT-MUST-BE-THERE

✵

A chapter where Grace is often alarmed and uncomfortable, and realises there is more to woods and wonder than colourful scenes and friendly voices.

When the world above was busy well before dawn
Heartsease woke Grace from a dream that whirled her
towards flickering lights down a round, rocky tunnel.
The only light now was a purply-white shimmer
of pale, luminous flowers bathed in moonshine.
It came from the guardian's garment that rustled
like leaves in a breeze as they wound their way down
below the main entrance to another long passage
that ran under Woodmaster's grove and the pond,
veering sharply away from the gate Grace had opened
with joy only to lose sight of Downcast Don;
and as they turned, a harsh draught whipped
her face, smoky dampness filled the air,
and a pinpoint of faint light showed ahead.
Soon they climbed rock-hewn stairs that suddenly
levelled into thick, coarse grass and reeds.
Looking back Grace saw no entrance, not even
a hole, just the wide arms of a distant wood.

The-Wood-That-Is-Not-There still looked inviting
as they left it further behind and moved swiftly
along a rough track on top of a muddy causeway
through a marsh stretching far and wide on each side.
Ahead was another wood. Alders and willows
that hung from its outer edge or seemed to wade
in filthy water looked straggly or almost dead.
Heartsease seemed at home here and somehow made them
float along, the way you walk in some dreams
without a footfall. Wonder stone showed
no ripple on its dark face. They passed through
clouds of gnats and mosquitoes whose wailing sounded
like a mournful song in a lost language.
In the wood brambles, hawthorn and holly looked
livelier than its lanky trees, but among them stood
a huge, grey-green ash. As old as Woodmaster,
though *he* was like an ancient building, not a ruin.

The ash had several rotten arms but held up one,
proud of its shiny, dancing leaves. A gaping hole
where a branch had fallen away from the trunk
looked like an empty eye socket. From it
sprang a spotted woodpecker, which cackled at
the strangers and screamed away into the echoing wood.
Grace was surprised that neither tree nor bird
had a word to say; and Heartsease was thoughtful.
Did she want her companion just to look and listen?

Fat-stalked ivy hugged the ash trunk
as if to suck its life away. Insects large and small
crawled over and burrowed into its bark. Hornets
droned in and out of a wide crack. They sounded
angry and threatening. Perched on a rotten twig
a grey-brown robin-like bird piped and piped,
zee-took, zee-took, dived down to catch flies
with a sharp snap, then back it came to pipe
and pipe, until a rush of wings, beak and talons
shot from trees beyond, and in the time it took
Grace to breathe twice, seized the small piper
and vanished into shadow, leaving only a few
downy feathers floating towards the forest floor.
'The cunning, stealthy hawk that strikes from any angle,'
said Heartsease. 'Here come black wood ants,
marching home to mounds of mashed leaf and stalk.'
Some left their queue to prod the useless feathers,
and scurried back as if they'd wasted precious time.

Seeing all this at once and so quickly
felt like looking through a magnifying glass,
and the amethyst reflected Grace's wonder
with swirling, snaky patterns; but where was her guide?

Nowhere to be seen or heard. Alone
and fearing the wood's strangely loud busyness,

all she could do was follow a rough path
that twisted on under clumps of trees, crowded
together as if fighting over the best places to live,
while bushes and shrubs grew thick and fast everywhere,
smothered saplings, and let nothing and no one pass through.
If only she could reach the well and start her journey
to the forge, away from a place where everything
had a wild, lively time except for trees.
Though it was hard to think they had feelings:
their hanging branches clawed at her face;
they tripped her up with long bony roots,
or dripped sticky mess onto her hat and dress.

Then as she wondered why Heartsease could glide
past every obstacle, the path dipped and ended
by a deep pool. It smelt stronger than compost
rotting and steaming on a hot summer's day,
its face was black, oily and scarred with fallen
leaves, twigs and stalks. She thought back to
the soft green mantle on Water Lily's bright pond.
The sun had broken through its shroud of mist
but little stirred in or around this still water.

A few flies see-sawed high up
as if on invisible strings but without
the faintest hum, and whatever dripped or dropped
from overhanging branches set off
a tiny spinning circle that upset and scattered
the flies until it spread out and died away.
Grace felt as though she might have been watching
a metal sheet deliberately painted black
to reflect no light, shapes or colours.

All she could do was follow a rough path that twisted on under clumps of trees, crowded together as if fighting over the best places to live…

The longer she looked, the surer she felt the pool was once
a deep pit where people dug and delved for something
they needed. She knew about old quarries and mines.
But just then a small striped snake wriggled away
from thick undergrowth and slipped into the water,
followed by a rat who plunged in after it.
In a moment the reptile stiffened, gave up
its looping swim and floated like old rope.
And the hungry rat spun round and round,
lay on its back as if gasping for air, sank
then rose to float just below the pond's skin
as if lurking and ready to grab its prey.
Time for Grace to pick her way carefully past
this poisonous watery cavern, scrambling over
cast-up rocks and heaps of yellow gravelly soil
until at last she plunged into a dark grove
of twisted yews, glad to tread their dry needles,
though pale toadstools were all that lit her way.

Turning the last corner of a long corkscrew path
and dazzled by daylight, she blundered through dusty webs
draped at the mouth of this tunnel to trap insects
that made for its warmth and shelter. But beyond
there opened up a place more cheerful and lively
than anywhere she'd been since leaving the first wood:
a wide bowl whose rocky sides were covered
by scrub oak and yellow-flowered gorse and broom.
Birches and alders hiding warblers that sang as they fed
stood in carpets of thick grass and countless flowers.
Water roared and twisted down from a sheer cutting
far ahead, rushed past, then turned aside from
the broken woods behind. Could that foaming mass
end up in the desolate marsh she'd crossed?
Grace felt sure she must follow the wild water
uphill and make for the narrow cleft it made

in the rocky wall, and then she heard a voice
that sang in tune and time with the bubbling stream.

She remembered the chant that seemed to rise up
from violets below the orchard hedge at home,
and in wonder clutched her amethyst:
it was marble-white but marked with purple streaks
as if to greet the return of Heartsease in song,
which sounded something like this to Grace:
Among violets, white but purple-veined,
    I've waited for you.
Tending white violets purple-stained
    I wait to guide you.
Watching her violets white and purple-grained
    Your guide awaits you.
But neither guardian nor violets were to be seen,
so she walked on upstream towards the falls
that plunged and tumbled down the deep-walled crevice.
The path grew steep, slippery and so narrow
she had to put one foot in front of another
and cling to hanging stems of fern and rowan tree.

She felt spray on her face and smelt the weed-strewn rocks,
which somehow gave her strength to climb on until
the greeny-white storm roared and churned far below
and she looked back and saw a rainbow flicker
in the mist of water drops, like a bridge
that swayed and sparkled high above the racing falls.
So what was real or unreal, she asked herself?
'Discover the real world,' Don had said before
he held her stone and saw the lively, beckoning wood.

The second wood was 'real' enough and yet she'd learned
to wonder even more, as if it had prepared her
to make the best of stranger places that lay ahead.
Her stone was layered into thin hoops, white

at the top, then passing from palest mauve to purple
so deep it might have been dark blue.
And now she had reached the top of the valley
the busy stream gurgled unseen far down
a crack that sliced through a marshy green carpet.

Further on she came to a grassy mound overshadowed
by spreading poplars that sighed and hissed, so tall
it strained her neck to look for their distant tops.
And here just above the invisible stream
grew hundreds of white violets. Among them
stood Heartsease with the Pedlar of Dreams who'd piped her
dreaming into the river town and summoned insects
to string a rainbow bridge over the bleak water.
Two smiling friends she was delighted to meet.

'You need another dream!' laughed the cheerful pedlar,
preparing his soft-toned, ebony pipe.
All this rough and tumble among trees and rocks!
A gentle melody will soothe you on your quest.'
'Rest here and breathe in the violet scent,'
said the guardian. 'Then you'll find the forge
to help poor Don. The way's been roundabout,
but as you climbed your thoughts and questions made me think
you'll soon see why.'
Grace was far from sure.

VIII

WELL

✵

Once more Grace finds a dream that leads her to another testing place, and as darkness looms, everyone who's there to help is cheerful and hopeful; but can she be?

As Grace lay and listened to the pedlar pipe
his melody, the shiny spade-like poplar leaves
whispered in time and seemed to sing: *Promises,*
promises: a silver spade to help Don dig
and find his gift of wonder. The piper's tunic
turned to leaves, and among them the guardian's mantle
divided into clumps of gold and purple flowers
whose way of looking at her never stayed the same
until they seemed to close their eyes, inviting her
to join them in a deep sleep and then to dream.
Or was she dreaming? It was dark but the place
felt like the first wood, calm and welcoming.
Not a ragged wood that made her feel like a stranger,
with no business to be there. Here she knew
Heartsease was close by, and all at once
a glowing yellowy mist arose from rows of candles
strangely still and carried by upright ladybirds.
Trees looked autumnal, their trunks like pillars of sand.

Here were the guardian's uniformed attendants
holding little poles dipped in that shining mixture
Grace had asked about when it boiled and frothed
in the underground kitchen. And soon the lights
showed a clearing ahead. She felt rustling leaves
give way to long grass, and bracken brushed her legs,
and not far off glimmered a circle of mossy stones
covered here and there by ferns and creeping ivy.
At last she'd reached the well top. Over it hung
an old willow that sheltered those who drew water.
Every year its new branches could be woven
into baskets, lined with clay, lowered and raised
by ropes from the same strong, springy wood.
Lamp bearers surrounded the wall to help

Grace find her way. She looked over the edge
at the rough stony shaft going down and down,
its sides bristling with plants that loved shadow and damp,
waiting for her to plunge past into darkness.

So far down! How lonely it would be!
Turn back now and she would break her promise.
The gift of wonder was hers and Don had nothing like it.
She clasped her stone to remember her good fortune,
and when she opened her palm the jewel glowed pale violet,
outshining the lamps that now looked to Grace like stalks
of glowing yellow mullein. She saw Heartsease smile
with encouragement, take a silver horn
from her robe to blow a note so high
it sounded like a faint whistle that set off
a slithering rush of countless feet, and a chorus
of rustling little voices. As the guardian promised,
the green folk would be here to help Grace descend.
They looked like spikes of dew-drenched grass
that had suddenly decided to march away,
and they knew what to do, working faster than
the human eye could follow, even by the light
from the jewel, lamps and a faint hint of dawn.

More than a hundred prepared a willow basket,
lined with silky seedhead tufts of Traveller's Joy
collected by hundreds more. Two hundred
tied on four willow twig ropes, shouted for
another hundred to lift it over the shaft lip,
ready for Grace to take her place and her chance.
Held steady in four places, and slowly lowered,
she would drop without nudging the rough stones.
And all the while these quick little workers teased
and pushed each other as if it were a game.
Some slipped over the well edge but clung to plants
or moss and scrambled back with a wave and a chuckle,

which somehow made Grace feel more at ease
as she climbed down into her swaying seat,
though there was still the dark unknown below.
'Goodbye and good luck!' said Heartsease,
gently touching the traveller's shoulder.
'It's just a long short cut to make you wiser!

You may meet a cousin of mine down there.
She's as old as the world, large as life
but larger. Greet her with my love and respect.
We share so much though our paths seldom cross.'
'I won't forget,' said Grace, afraid she'd never
return to tell her guide she'd kept her word.
'Hold tight!' cried the restless sea of green,
as all its tiny figures strained at once to lower
the heavy wickerwork. 'Keep your spirits up!'
cried the leaders. 'We'll be here and all ready
to heave you back to the clearing in this wood
we're told is neither here nor there; but who cares!'
The first light of dawn touched Grace's hat
as they reeled her down below the parapet.
The grey circle above shrunk and she clung
to what seemed like her cage, though lantern poles
stuck between its woven sticks lit up the shaft.
The ladybird attendants had not forgotten her.

Ferns seemed to bow as she passed them,
and glossy green creepers glad of company
wanted to shake her hand. This must be
an important person coming down with lights
and overlooked by armies of anxious green folk,
now invisible to Grace as she sank
slowly down, then with a jolt stuck fast
on a stone loosened by some watercourse
that made a shiny pool in the well wall.

Here a lonely tadpole floated to and fro
and made a squeaky request: '*Skwill you skelp
the skelpless* !' 'What could I do for you?'
asked Grace in disbelief. (Frogs creak and croak
but aren't tadpoles dumb little blobs with tails?)
'*When you skramble back I skall be a frog.
Skwill you skoop me up and skelp me to the wood*?'
Such forethought from a tiny amphibian!
(she could hear dear distant Aunt Miriam talking!)
'Of course!' said Grace, like a fine lady used to
handing out favours from her open carriage.
'Perhaps you can help, too. I must find
Mighty Smith and his blazing forge.' '*Easky*!'
chuckled the tadpole with a twinkle in its tail.
'*Your bucket'll sklosh in the cold, cold pool.
Skpring out, skwerve right, neskt left,
skekond on your right. Skeep leaping on
till you skmell fire and skeer skammering.
Won't go askstray now, skhey*?!' it squealed
and turned a somersault. Grace wanted to ask
how it kept so cheerful halfway down a well,
but the rope team suddenly edged her away
and faster down until she hit the bubbling spring,
leapt on to a rocky shelf, dragged the basket
to safety, and took two candle poles to find her way
through the tunnels ahead. She stopped to take a breath:
how *could* she have done all that so easily?

IX

FORGE

A chapter where Grace is surprised by how much skilful work is swiftly and happily done in dark places, but making the spade she needs is not so easy.

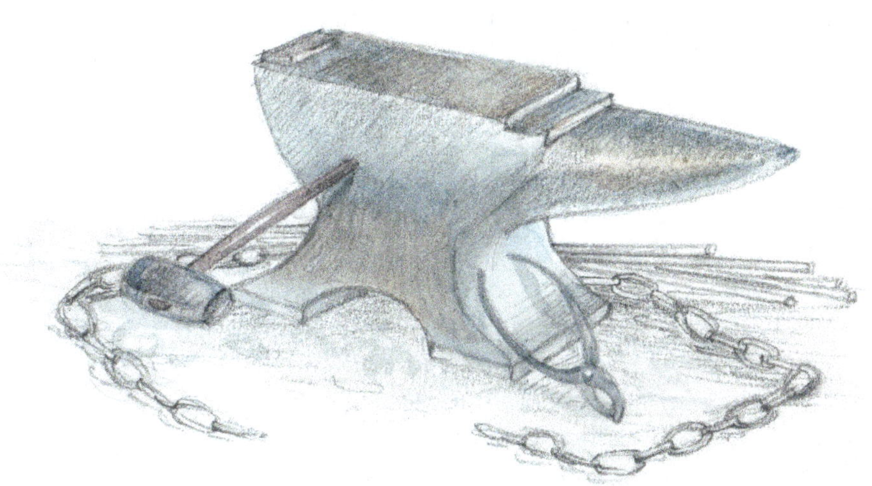

The passages were high and wide, layered with patterns
glistening in the torch light. Roof and walls
oozed and dripped into puddles she had to wade through.
Maybe the smithy fire would dry her dress and shoes
as it did on rain-soaked walks to and from school.
She stuck to what the tadpole had told her, thankful
for its lefts and rights through this maze of tunnels,
and after the last turning her poles went dim
in a dancing blaze of distant firelight. She heard
the clink-clunk of countless hammers on metal.
In wonder that at last the smoky forge was near
she clutched her stone and found its purple face alight
with white flames, just as she entered a high cavern
leading to a great archway that seemed to be on fire.
The forge furnace in the cave beyond was surely
ten times larger and hotter than any she'd seen at home.
The strangely small figures inside were too busy
in all that smoke and heat to pay attention to Grace.

She ventured to look round an entrance pillar
but there was no sign of the Great Smith
(who was working alone at an intricate necklace).
And what she did see made her try hard
not to giggle. The hammerers she'd heard were nine
dwarfs, broad and strong but much shorter than her,
all alike and tapping a sheet of red-hot metal
rata-tata, turn and turn about, in perfect time.
Though they all looked up at her, one by one,
each with one wide eye above his nose,
not for a moment did they pause for breath.
A comic sight, but she must not hurt their feelings.
In a loud voice she asked the nearest dwarf his name.
'Round-Eye-One' was all he'd time to shout.

'Perhaps you are brothers?' she asked very politely.
'What are the others called?' 'Round-Eye-Two

and so on up to Nine,' grunted One, striking
his one-ninth share without missing a single blow.

'Please tell me why you have only one
large eye?'(Should she have asked this?)
All nine looked up and stared severely,
not of course stopping their endless *clinkity-clunk*,
while Round-Eye-One declared: 'it takes one eye
to see our work. Two might show us folk who choose
to laugh at how we look and what we have to do.'
Grace felt well and truly put down
and thought it time and tactful to change the subject.

'Is the Mighty Smith anywhere to be found?'
One cheered up: 'Certainly, my dear!'
His eye spun with sparks like a Catherine wheel
and his smile so nearly sliced his face in two.
Grace felt she'd burst if she didn't laugh,
but to hide this she looked around the forge
and studied what the dwarfs were beating into shape:
a suit of armour that flickered with pale blue light
as it mirrored the great fire's spurting flames.

Round-Eye-One called a halt and stopped his brothers
like a machine. Taking mugs numbered One to Nine
from a shelf, they dipped them in a foaming tub,
drank slow draughts, then without a word
took out little books and lost themselves in reading.
The steel suit looked so delicate and fragile
Grace had to ask: 'What is that made of?'
'Moonlight,' said One, still ready to talk,
and he really seemed to mean what he said.

Or did it stand for something else? 'Made for
a knight known as Sir Cloudy Lost-Heart,
or, more respectably, Sir Substantial-Nebule.

A man of substance but as easy to pin down
as a cloud: hence nebule (once *nebulous*)
d'you see?' Grace didn't but nodded politely.
'Still, he's a genial fellow and pays well.
Castle in the Air's his home. Mostly he wanders
here, there and everywhere. *Cloudy,* d'you see?!'

'If only I could visit him on my way to
the Rainbow!' One had no idea what she meant
and said: 'Take a look round our forge, the finest
you'll ever see, and no smith equals *the* Smith
in strength and skill. Your man for massive tasks
or jobs so finicky they'd tie your fingers in knots.'
'When will he appear?' asked Grace, wondering
if he was hard to catch like the cloudy knight.
'He's linking up a spell-binding necklace
ordered by Sir Cloudy. *Sir Beck-and-Call*
if you ask me!' So she'd have to wait.

Waiting or taking long short cuts took up
much of her journey. Perhaps to find and cross the Rainbow
you learnt and wondered about every kind of colour.
And that far-off morning, as it now seemed,
the flower guardians had shown her that colour
was far more than shades and tones you happened to like.
Stray thoughts Grace tried hard to fit together.

All at once the dwarfs clattered back to work,
which gave her time to explore the vast workshop.
First she counted twenty-seven pairs of bellows
that heaved and puffed whenever the fire lost heat
without anyone stopping work to pump them.
Along the walls hung a wonderful array
of objects cunningly made from iron, steel,
brass, every kind of alloy and precious metal:
axes, buckles, badges, bolts, chains, charms

knives, locks, pincers, saws. Think from A
to Z and you'd find something perfect there.
Like the furnace and bellows, everything had powers,
for the Smith's craft came from deep knowledge
of all that can happen and lie hidden when air,
fire, molten metals and skill are bound together.
Grace felt enchanted, grasped her amethyst
and found it splashed with gleaming tongues of sapphire
like wind-torn crests of waves on a violet sea.

Intent on this and now further from the firelight,
she nearly fell over the Smith who always sat
cross-legged on the floor to do minute work.
He was far too bulky to sit at a bench.
First she noticed his great red and gold beard,
so furnace-like it could be on fire,
and seemed to cover his face like a balaclava.
Then she saw his long, surprisingly slender fingers
and sensed their cleverness. Across them lay a garland,
woven from finest metals, glinting sunlight yet gleaming
with subtle moonlight, and when Smith lifted it
the silver celandines, buttercups and primroses
crackled and rustled like shaken leaves. His task was over,
and to Grace's disappointment, he tucked it away
in a deep pocket, took off the woollen cap
he wore to hold in his wild hair, bowed and got up.
He was so slowly and was so huge she began to wonder
if he would ever stand up straight in this cavern.

His eyes reminded Grace of giant-oak Woodmaster:
they took note of her slowly and kindly, made her
feel at ease despite his overwhelming size,
even when she gave him her hand in greeting
and saw it vanish as if never to be returned.
'Rare to see a lady here!' He laughed so loudly
it sounded like a horse-drawn coach racing over cobbles.

'So what can I, of all folk, do for you?'
Grace looked all the way up to his scruffy,
questioning face, and felt calm and confident,
somehow feeling sure he'd understand her need:
'I've been told to ask for a silver spade.
Downcast Don has never learned to wonder,
or had a gift like my stone.' (She opened her palm
and it shone so brightly Smith raised his eyebrows!)
'Heartsease, my guide, says he'd dig and dig
and discover so much to wonder about he'd want
to find and cross the Rainbow, just like I do.'

...she saw his long, surprisingly slender fingers and sensed their cleverness. Across them lay a garland woven from finest metal...

Slow-moving, deep-thinking Smith looked
the long way down to Grace, stroking and tugging at
his thick, fiery beard. The One-Eyes so rarely saw
their master look taken aback, they stopped work,
and the only sound in that deep-down forge
was the bellows forcing the fire to wake up.
The giant craftsman paced round his walls, followed
by Grace, who noticed steel bows with sheaves of arrows,
so slender and tough they'd fly right over a hill,
ladders that could unfold to scale the tallest towers,
bells made to stay sound and ring true for ever,
but not a simple silver spade for Don to use.
'None to be found, though I've made many,'
said the Smith, who liked to help his visitors.
'Perhaps you could make me one in no time,'
suggested Grace. 'Trouble is,' said Smith, 'we need
special silver ore. Nothing else will do,
as it won't carry the power to charm the digger.

The mine's small and owned by someone
who's part of the wide world and its long making.
I've used up the lump she last allowed me.
We're terribly busy here and she can take days
to accept our needs. Suppose you ask her
for just enough to sift and smelt into a spade:
she'll surely agree. And it's quite near.'
(*Close by or not: who knows?* thought Grace,
I'll just have to make for wherever it is.)

'What should I call this ancient person?' she asked
'Depends,' said Smith, as if talking to himself.
'She's beyond naming, though some have tried
and she doesn't mind. But 'old' offends her,
sounds as if she's worn out and won't last.
Try *Earth-Wise, Rock-Heart, Span-Seer,*
Age-Dweller, Time-Queller, Ore-Dealer…

'Isn't this the cousin Heartsease mentioned?' asked Grace.
I know they seldom meet but are they quite alike?'

'That's too much!' roared the Smith, his laughter
shaking all those precious items on the walls.
Even the One-Eyes joined him in short bursts.
'My turn to be laughed at, I suppose,' said Grace.
''Fraid so,' Smith admitted, tapping her shoulder
very gently with one finger. 'Don't worry.
Our Stone-grown Lady of Desert Places will not
say *No* to an adventurous little person
who wields a wonder jewel.' 'Where will I find
her house?' And they all laughed even louder.
'House? You think *I'm* very large,' shouted Smith.
'She's so vast she lives, or lies, half buried
in a wide sandy place. You can't miss her.'
With that he moved Grace towards the forge door.
The One-Eyes waved farewell with their nine hammers,
one by one. 'Follow your nose. You can't go wrong.
We'll expect you back quite soon.'(No directions!
and so far down just to be sent further on.)

X

ANCIENT ROCK-HEART

✵

Grace has her strangest encounter so far but she is bravely determined to make the most of this meeting.

Grace had forgotten her lamp poles and soon
the forge light faded; the passage closed in,
twisting and turning, and she had to blunder on
in total dripping darkness until a strange blue glow
showed ahead and lit the rough damp walls
with strands of rainbow. It came from a side chamber
cut into the rock, high and vaulted, covered
with coloured, patterned tiles and dazzling crystal shapes.
Four figures sat round a smokeless fire
whose blue flames leapt from rocks in a stone hearth.
Each watcher's silken cloak was embroidered
with its own letter: ***N, E, S, W,***
coloured to match their long, contrasting hair:
ginger-red, raven, nut-brown, flaxen-fair.
Where they men or women? Grace couldn't tell.
They tended fire from earth's core. Among others
Smith could light tapers here, which meant his furnace
burnt hotter and rarely needed a rake and clean.

Somehow knowing not to disturb the still guardians,
Grace strode on and climbed steeply towards
a great archway full of broad daylight. It opened
onto a sandy plain stretching far and wide,
a vast Nowhere that made her feel a tiny speck.
Glancing back to the crown of the arch
she noticed a circular sculpture: four heads
seen from above faced out four ways
as if they covered every compass point between them.

Not much use to her, she thought: a desert
in front, a tunnel behind, and no bearings to follow.
Rubbing her stone in surprise and puzzlement
she found it pale and blank like the view before her.
Yet far across the sand she thought she could see
two peaks like mountains built from stone blocks,
unless it was a mirage, and then a huge shadow fell

across her. The largest woman known to the world
loomed up like a rocky precipice.

She sat motionless in the sand, arms folded,
her chin resting on them as she gazed out
across the desert and up at the high sun.
She seemed to be deep in thought or remembering
matters far back in time. *Rock-Heart*, thought Grace,
if that was what to call her when asking a favour.
Could she have missed seeing someone like this?
Maybe those distant peaks moved and planted themselves
next to her with one or two invisible strides.

How could she be heard from so far below?
Was this mountainous being cousin to Heartsease?
Her face reminded Grace of a church tower
glimpsed through mist: you found eyes, ears
a gargoyle nose and a gaping mouth,
or did you? As it was, the ancient being
took no notice of the girl who was about
the size of a snail to her. 'How do I ask
for silver so Smith can make Don's precious spade',
she wondered, looking at the large bare feet
half buried in sand. And then she saw some steps
that ran up and over the crags and crevices
of this living mass of stone, and round her neck.
She must climb, and quickly, not to waste her trek.
The path was steep and had no rail but she ran
as if her feet were winged and she were weightless,
and soon passed below the staring eyes and on
towards a gigantic sea-shell ear.

She whispered: 'Please will you give me a lump of ore
so Smith can make a silver spade for Downcast Don?'
How this mighty building of a person jumped to hear
such words without a warning! But only slowly did her head

rise with a creak from its pillow of folded arms,
shake from side to side and shout, 'No!' And with that
her whole body became once more as rigid
as mountainside under your feet.

'All this way
to be turned down by a stubborn old rock!'
Grace walked impatiently round the stone collar
beneath the weathered lumpy grey face, looked up
at the unblinking eyes which reminded her
of deep, dark pools that never mirrored the sky;
serious, yet somehow content and peaceful.
Had they looked over countless miles of desert
for thousands of years, or had she seen change after
change until the land became this dry and empty?
Such thoughts then brought Heartsease to mind.

She recalled the strange gaze that saw beyond
the words she was speaking and assured you
that everything made sense, however odd it felt.
Cousins then? Perhaps! Grace crept back
to the shell-like ear and spoke more boldly:
'My guide and guardian Heartsease told me to greet you
if we happened to meet.' '*A GREETING FROM HER!*'
The misshapen stony mass stirred, tightened
and looked like some ancient warrior queen, strong
in body and will. Yet the voice was as rich and deep
as the notes of a church organ's largest pipes.
'And you took the trouble to bring word of her!'
boomed the Desert Queen. 'Answer a question
and you may have whatever you ask me for.
Be thankful it's not a riddle, but my questions
have to be answered backwards. Walk three times
round my neck and you'll find what you're after
written on my back. 'I'll try my best,' said Grace.

She squeezed her stone as if to ask it for help.
It looked blank and would have shrugged its shoulders
if stones could do so. 'Well then!' hummed the giantess,
her eyes fixed beyond the parched sea of sand.
'What don't I have that Heartsease doesn't either?'
Put like that it was doubly puzzling to Grace.
She walked behind the great neck and under a mass of hair
like wiry heather clinging to the crown of a hill,
then saw something that brought to mind
a pattern behind and below her guardian's garments,
luminous slender leaves delicately veined,
rather like long, thin crescent moons,
apart from the fabric yet floating within it.
Something similar hovered over this rocky back,
as if rippling water threw patterns of light
onto a smooth stone arch. Really these were
airy antennae that sent and received news,
which is why very little surprised these cousins.

Grace walked three times round and began to wonder
if these leafy figures belonged without belonging.
'I want a one-word answer,' the throbbing voice demanded.
Leaves seemed the nearest, so she took a chance.
'Right first time and no guesses. I'm pleased!
Learning to wonder's taught you more than you think.
Now climb into my pocket and fetch a lump of ore.
I've just brought it from that far-off mountain mine.'
The pocket was a cave, damp and full of echoes,
but she soon stumbled over the glistening silver ore,
surely from those odd peaks: they weren't a mirage
and couldn't have been Rock-Heart seen from miles away.
That mighty being's head was once again
at rest on folded arms. She'd spoken more
than suited her. But wonder stone's mood had changed:
its surface shone flinty silver over purple depths

that flickered in and out of many shades. Time for
Grace to climb lightly down to the sand.

Quickly finding the arch below hills that dropped
to desert, she trusted her feet and plunged back
into narrowing darkness. What about the blue light
of earth fire and its watchers in that vaulted hall?
No time to wonder, for soon a forge glow
lit up and gave shape to the wet, slimy tunnel.
Smith, who seemed to know she was on her way,
was waiting and welcomed her back with a careful pat
on the shoulder. The dwarfs were grinning from ear to ear.

XI

WELCOME BACK

A chapter where Grace returns to woodland light to rest briefly from her travels and celebrate what she has so far done, only to be told how much more there is to learn and achieve.

Grace was told to sit on a four-legged stool
and left to rest or watch while Smith and his dwarfs worked
at breakneck speed. But her old friend One
did pour out a mug of their foaming drink
to give her strength for the journey back to the wood.
It smelt of mint and lavender, and tasted sweeter
than rich honey, warming her from throat to toes
after the damp, cold tunnel, though she soon felt
the power of the fire fanned to white heat
by twenty-seven pairs of bellows. They knew
what had to be done to help the craftsmen
who smelted the ore and blended precious silver
with finely tempered steel ready to be forged into
a spade. And Smith and the Round-Eyed gang mixed,
hammered and shaped so rapidly without once
getting in each other's way, it seemed to Grace
no more than a couple of minutes before
Don's fine new spade sizzled in the cooling tank.

Soon it was ready to have its Y-shaped handle
bolted on. 'DD' was finely hatched into
its burnished shaft, and the blade perfectly honed.
Smith handed the gift to her handle first,
pleased with a task well done. At last
Grace could return with her promise fulfilled,
and she was almost too glad and thankful to speak.
The craftsman knew this and said: 'No need
for thanks. It's in your eyes. Your patience won
the spade-making. We always like to be busy.'
What could he give her, he wondered. Going through
thick and thin should be handsomely rewarded.
He reached high among his smaller priceless treasures
and found a belt that might have been made for Grace.
Woven into it were gems that shone with rosy light.
'Wear this and you won't be in the dark. No more

stumbling clueless along murky passageways!
Mind you: there *are* worse kinds of darkness.'

Smith placed the weightless present around her waist
and buckled it as if he were threading a needle.
Then he took both her hands in his and bowed
while the one-eyed dwarfs removed their work caps,
scraping the forge floor one after the other.
So Grace left carrying a wonder gift, blessed
with powers to start Don on his own journey,
at least as long as hers, though never quite the same.
Her belt lit up the winding passages
and led her to the rocky quay beside the spring
at the bottom of the well vent. Suppose
her friends above had given up and left her
with a damp basket and heavy spade to shout
up the shaft like an unanswered echo.
The willow bucket seat was at least hanging ready,
its four twig ropes going up and up until
they vanished towards the far-off, invisible
daylight and the woodlands she longed to see.

If she climbed in and made the spade secure,
the green spear folk might be aware of her.
And at once there was a sudden twitch through
the ropes; they took the strain and up she went…

If she climbed in and made the spade secure,
the green spear folk might be aware of her.
And at once there was a sudden twitch through
the ropes; they took the strain and up she went slowly
but surely. How about that waiting tadpole, she wondered.
It was a frog now and leapt off the ledge
into the basket without a by-your-leave,
but it had lost the squeaky, skittish tadpole talk.
'Heavy to carry, that spade!' 'It's not for me
but for a friend in need,' said Grace and told
the tale of how Downcast Don longed to wonder.
That impressed the frog, who promised to help the boy.
'I'll surprise him with a thing or two. I've a list
of wonders as long as all my legs put together.
He'll turn these up with his spade once he's learnt
to trust what Dame Nature says, like it or not.'
They were almost up. The frog had had his say,
hopped onto the rocky parapet and vanished.

When the basket was at last level with the wall,
Grace felt a time shift had taken place:
before she was lowered down, flowers and birdsong
spoke of early summer. Somehow it now felt
long past midsummer, that in-between
season Grace had learnt to call the lattermath.
She was even more sure of this when Heartsease,
who'd helped the green army with its heavy task,
welcomed her in a gown that had changed
from purple to yellow. Just like her namesakes who grow
paler and give their seedlings the same dress.
'Back to woodland light!' said the guardian.
'I needn't tell you how glad we are. Your powers
of wonder have grown in darkness, firelight and desert,
and you've given a boy you didn't much care for a chance
to see this many-coloured world for what it is.

Let's celebrate until you complete this task
with a visit to Dame Nature, Mother of Guardians.'

Heartsease took the silver spade and laid it flat
for a host of green spear folk to carry
as if this was their trophy and triumph.
And the smartly dressed ladybirds followed
three by three. It was a long, slow procession
to the great elm, below whose massive trunk
lay the entrance to the guardian's night-time home.
Walking behind near her guide Grace was filled
with a warm rush of relief from head to toe:
she was back where leaves danced and sang
while the green band swayed along and added
base and treble. And were there ever such flowers
in the dappled sunlight of a woodland floor,
she wondered, thinking back to Smith's stifling forge
and Old Rock-Heart's parched, empty wilderness.
Meanwhile, the march must have been long and slow
for the westering sun reddened and began to sink
when they slipped below the elm canopy
and the gnarled bark door flew open.

The energetic tribes of green-grass folk
somehow melted away into the evening shadows
leaving the silver spade for ladybirds to carry.
Grace felt sorry she'd had not time to thank them.
She did not mind going underground again,
for this sloping hallway and the fire-lit room
beyond were not dark like the tunnels and caves
below the deep well. They reminded her
of how she could close her eyes and hide away
for comfort in a warm embrace from Aunt Miriam.
Into the rocky walls were fixed those strange poles
dipped in luminous mixture that still bubbled
away in its pot beside the cooking fire.

The gems in the Smith's belt flashed and sparkled and all
admired their young guest's finely crafted gift.
And on the rough table was spread a feast
prepared by Heartsease and her uniformed helpers
ready for the traveller's safe, successful return.

Grace was amazed by such a welcome. Her stone
had turned to whitest quartz and its crystal seams
matched the undersides of mushrooms piled in bowls
and ready to be eaten along with spotted woodland fungi,
hazelnuts, clover-scented honeycombs, wild cherries,
strawberries and jugs of light-bearing brew,
the same one made to test colours and paint lamp-poles.
One small mug of this 'wondershine',
as she called it, quenched her thirst and filled her mind
and body with many day- and night-time
smells and sights of the late-summer woods above.
And while they ate and drank the spade stood shining
in a corner, and she described the rapid work
that Smith and his dwarves put into its making.
'Now he'll be Delver Don!' laughed Heartsease,
'or more likely *Delighted* Don, no longer
Downcast, because he'll discover more and yet
more that will make him wonder about the earth.

But *The-Wood-That-Is-Not-There* is closed to him
till other guardians and their helpers take you
to meet Dame Nature, who will show Don
how to make best use of his spade.'
'Where must I go?' asked Grace, who felt
she'd done enough exploring and did not want
to think beyond this happy, comfortable moment.
No well-shafts, caverns or dried-up deserts, she hoped.
'At dawn after a long rest you'll come across
a place where trees give way to open ground
that climbs towards a hill covered with gorse and broom,

one of many hills that house and shelter those called Primers, Painters and Protectors, who help care for plants in every season. Lively, cheerful spirits that look as flimsy as flower petals, and you may just see straight through them! Guardians like me direct their work. Watching it you'll learn more about colour: part of your rainbow journey.

'But how can I get inside a hill?' asked Grace. 'Approach and you'll hear music in the air, and you must reply with these simple verses that show you'd like to see and understand this work.

Spirits who colour and care,
always busy, never still,
may I visit your hill?
Spirits who prime, paint,
and watch, I'll wait until
you lead me under your hill.
Spirits who flit and fly
beyond our sight, what will
I learn inside your hill?

Not very colourful words perhaps, but sung in a high, sweet voice, they sounded to Grace like a spell, and easy to recall.
'If I say that will they let me in?'
'Yes,' said her guide, 'if you're loud and clear!'

XII

COLOURFUL CARE

❋

A chapter where we follow Grace under hill to learn new ways of looking at the seasons and their colours as she completes the last part of her promise to Don.

At sunrise two silent ladybirds showed Grace out
carrying Don's spade. When she looked back
there was no trace of the elm-trunk door.
Soon the wood thinned out and she walked up
a slope of thick grass and sedge leading to
a smooth-topped hill, its sides matted with dark-green bushes
just as Heartsease had described. But first
in the middle of this nowhere she found
a hedgeless field divided neatly into four:
fallow plough, green shoots, ripe barley,
prickly stubble. How could that be done?
And what was she supposed to think about it?
She'd got used to puzzles but here was one
that seemed to make perfect nonsense of the seasons
she was used to. Ah well: such neat and tidy work
mustn't be disturbed. She slipped past to one side.
A flock of rooks soared up from the plough furrows,
and without cark or caw vanished into thin air.

There followed a noise that mixed up well-known sounds:
a rising skylark, jingling harness, harsh wind,
heavy rain pattering on hard ground. No sooner
had she decided this than it ceased
and might never have been. She felt her spine tingle
and clutched the wonder stone only to find it showed
a chessboard pattern of tiny white and mauve squares.
As fast as the tussocky ground allowed she strode
to the hillside, ready to shout her well-learnt verses.

Gorse and broom had gone to seed but the ground
was covered with pink bindweed and purple harebells.
And then there was music, faint and far-off, under
the hill perhaps, or was it a wind-blown bush laden
with flutes and chimes? Sombre at first, it burst
into a dance that clashed and thumped through the morning air
and somehow made Grace feel ready to take

any chance that came her way. She held her stone
tightly, tucked the shining spade to her side,
and proclaimed her verses to the bushes and flowers
who had nothing to say in return, but there followed
a loud blast from all over the hillside
like the blaring of a hundred and one trumpets,
though no such instruments were at work:
earth spirits had welcomed her through
all those cornet-shaped bind weed flowers, and once
they'd sounded off, a wide green gate unfolded
between the bushes as if had always stood there.

Waiting just inside was a tall guardian
Grace recalled from that morning in her bedroom
when colourful figures offered their gifts.
Here was Deep-Pink Clover who'd not spoken
but listened with a smile to Camomile's words.
She wore a long mantle tinged with green strands.
Her face looked ready to joke and be light-hearted
but like Heartsease she had that uncanny way
of looking straight into your thoughts and beyond.

'I'm glad you're able to visit our hill.' Her voice
sounded all at once like linnets singing in flight
and a brook trickling over stony shallows.
'All will be pleased to see you, though you'll find
our spirits very busy. Only the wealthy
whose hearts are choked by their need to be wealthier
and those who've grown up without keeping their hearts
young cannot enter our working hills.
What would our care for growth and colour mean to them?'

'I've been sent to ask a favour,' said Grace politely,
relieved that she was one of the lucky ones allowed
to visit. 'I would like to meet Dame Nature.
I need her help and advice to complete my task,

or so my guide and guardian, Heartsease, tells me.'
This guardian looked pleased to be asked.
'It will be easy. Our Mother visits often
to look at our work. First I'd like to show you
some of the skills and concerns that keep us busy.

There are four kinds of spirits who help us
to fulfil what the four seasons require.
I'm mainly concerned with spring. My workers
appear to be clothed in deep pink like me.
'We're less busy now it's late summer:
our plants sleep their way towards new strength
in what some call Dame Nature's nursery.
Red Carnation directs the summer forces
who are away from our hill-halls ready
to defend flowers and shrubs from rogue gales
and trampling storms that pound and split them
when they are heavy with leaf, blossom and seed.
These helpers appear to be dressed in scarlet.
Autumn primers, painters and protectors are guided
by Marigold Amber who loves late flowers
and leaves about to fall. Bell of the woods
attends to winter colouring and care, but growth
from bulbs, corms and tubers concerns her most of all.

'Their teams are busy conjuring up what's needed
for the next seasons, and you may see their shapes
of yellowy-orange and dark blue preparing scenes
and testing ideas of what's best for their charges.
They picture settings and details to make sure everything
grows, goes to seed or sleeps as it should.
Unlike the artists you have seen at work
they sketch and colour to make the earth come alive,
and couldn't paint something that's already there.

'But here I am with summer time on my hands
and filling it with all this chatter. Please ask me
anything you'd like to know as we wander
through our under-hill workshops and studios.'
'Thank you for telling me so much,' said Grace.
My aunt and uncle taught me that living things
slowly but surely find ways to make themselves
stronger. But you show how love, care and skill
matter most. I like both ways
of looking at our colourful world. Both make me
clasp my stone in wonder till it sparkles
like sunlight dancing on water…' She paused
and thought: is it me talking like this?
It was as if she'd been in a dream
where you could be so much older and wiser.
'Will I see Nature's nursery?' she asked.
'You *may* if she feels it's right for you,' said Clover.
'Words don't matter to her; it's who you are.'

All the high, wide rooms Grace passed
seemed bright enough to be under a clear sky
and rustled and shimmered with restless shapes and shadows.
Some autumn helpers in their golden-orange cloaks,
each like a thousand fine petals sewn together,
seemed to be painting trees with gold and scarlet leaves,
darting among the branches on invisible ropes.
Despite their haste there were no spots or splashes,
and no sign of paint pots or dirty brushes.

Others opened late flowers as they painted:
chrysanthemums lit up in orange flames;
green knot-buds of tall michaelmas daisies
burst into purple dishes full of hover flies;
traveller's joy wrapped yellowing shrubs and hedges
with its seed-head shawls; blackberries turned
from hard unripe red to jet-black clusters, their skins

polished and shining in low autumnal sunlight.
So much colour and movement made you feel dizzy.

Elsewhere winter spirits in midnight blue
already planned the survival of plants,
making sure they would not be deceived by days
of spring warmth only to be blighted and blackened
by yet more icy winds and withering frosts.
Grace shivered at the many bleak pictures
unfolding, though she was amazed to discover
different kinds of holly with their glossy coats
and bright berries among icicles and snow drifts.

What about the fun and excitement of Christmas
made even better by heavy falls of snow?
No hint of that in these scenes that came alive
as unseen brushes painted airy canvases.
And while she watched the silver spade grew heavier.
'Sit and rest till Dame Nature arrives,' said Clover.
Dazed by all that flashed before her Grace was glad
to sit down beside her guide on mounds of moss,
though an endless, repeated chant filled the air.

Here we are to test it.
More and more to do,
never over is it?
So much and such and such to visit
think we'll ever get through it?
Tint, shine, splash and dye,
be sure to find the best.
Fidget, forage, flit and fly
till season's ready and lets us rest.

Cheerfully sung and to a simple tune:
Grace could have joined the frantic, busy chorus,

as Clover did in sweet, clear tones,
but maybe visitors should just listen.
It was a song to work to, and just as
she grew very tired of it she noticed something
move slowly towards them: a long blue ribbon
that every now and again rang with solemn bells.
Clover knew what it was: 'Harebells are troubled
and have formed a long procession in protest.'
It looked as if each one moved forward
little by little on its slender stem and shook
its bells in turn to make a mournful sound.
Huddled closer together and following behind,
some carried a large mallow leaf and on it
lay a small bunch of companions, wilted and dying.
The leaders stopped near Clover and one said:
'We'd like to see Dame Nature. Is she here?'

'We expect her soon,' said the guardian gently.
'But perhaps I can help you in some way.'
'I'm afraid not,' said the outspoken harebell.
Her voice sounded broken and forlorn. 'Some child
has probably picked our fellow plants, grown
tired of them, and left them to wither and die
beside a woodland path. We're meant to ring in
a festival of late summer fruitfulness,
but first we had to bring our neglected friends
to Nature's nursery.' Clover could only say:
'Spring will return and I'll make doubly sure
you're all back in force, blessing open spaces
with your airy bells.' To watch or listen to
such distress made Grace ashamed and tongue-tied.
How often had she picked wild flowers
for the sake of it and found she'd dropped them
when something else distracted her. What a relief
that just then Clover shouted: 'Here's Dame Nature!'

To Grace she seemed as old as ancient Rock-Heart
but tall and upright as a straight, young larch tree.
Oaks, mountains and waterways were no match
for her age and yet her deep blue eyes
were as clear and trouble-free as the girl's own,
because this Mother of Guardians never ceased
to wonder at the marvels of ever-changing Earth,
or put first and foremost her love and care for it
and anything, however small, that grew and lived on it.

Her cloak was a rich brown like moist soil and leaf-mould,
its green hood flickered through every shade
from dark yew to silvery-underleaf of aspen.
Below this she shone with flowers from all seasons,
and their fragrance was like a dewy May dawn.
Grace expected the harebells to cluster round
such life-giving presence. Where were they?
Did she dream about their mournful procession
and how they wanted to consult Dame Nature?
Perhaps she dozed off while sitting beside Clover,
strangely tired after watching the spirits at work.
But now the earth mother wanted to welcome her,
stooped down and held her close, which felt like
resting on new-mown hay full of countless scents.
'So you've found your way to me. I hoped you would.
I'm sure you've a query or a request. Most do!'
'One of each, please!' answered Grace who sensed
she was talking to someone who liked to listen.

'Will you show Downcast Don how to use
this silver spade?' she asked, lifting it up.
'It's to help him find out how to wonder.'
The answer came in a voice that sounded at once
amused, pleased and song-like. 'You've journeyed
through darkness, heat, and drought to win it for a boy
I know of. Thanks to the way you spoke he listened,

and like you he'd like to follow a path that leads to
the Rainbow, though he might not realise it!
And first he must open the earth and his mind
with a spade brought to him for selfless reasons.
But I know you want to ask something else.'
'Am I allowed to visit your nursery?'
'Of course!' said the kindly guardian, took the spade
in one hand and held her guest's in the other.
Grace turned to thank and say goodbye to Clover
but she needed to look over her sleeping charges
and followed down the steep spiral stairway.

In vaults lit mainly by the guardians' robes
many plants slept and recovered in soils
that suited them, so there was little to see
but the carers knew how to look out and correct
growth that was too fast or of the wrong kind.
It was still and peaceful: Nature and Clover moved
without a sound from one seed bed to another,
stooped lovingly to fold away a stray leaf
or cover a shoot too eager to find the light.

Grace was delighted to recognise speedwells
who'd encouraged her on the country lane
when others had been remote, proud or mocking.
They'd told her why she should travel on and on
and promised how this very visit would show her
nothing is ever lost or wasted. Summer spirits
had brought some plants back to strengthen them
for next spring. They were too sleepy to greet her
but she still recalled their songs and lively advice.

Perhaps the mournful harebells came down here
and put their sisters to rest, but when she told old Nature
what she thought she'd seen, the kindly guardian
smiled and raised a warning finger to her mouth;

though somewhere far away (or was it in her head?)
she heard some harebells chant this sombre little song:

Our sisters grew along a woodland way
until a careless hand
snatched them up in play

Once they rang their bells below the broomy hill.
Now shrunk and dry
their music's forever still.

They sang to every dawn and opened for the sun.
Did someone silence them
for just a moment's fun?

Let them sleep while children laugh and play.
Farewell bell-friends
until another summer's day.

Words that were set to a light-hearted tune,
which made Grace find them all the more moving.
Noticing this Nature said: 'Don't forget
that whatever happens every flower is cared for.
Even one harebell's life matters to us.'
'And spring's never far off,' whispered Clover,
not just to add some comfort. A tiny snowdrop
was about to push aside its earthy cover.
'Not yet! You're in a rush! Wait for
the best moment to make the world wonder
as you burst into life though frost and snow.'
Grace laughed. 'Thank you for this under-hill visit.
It has shown me new ways to look and listen.'
'You have the gift of wonder,' said old Nature.
'Earth will never begin to feel dull or stale.
Coming here seems another long way round

but learning not to take anything for granted
helps to guide you towards rainbow wisdom.'

'This may help, too,' said Clover. 'You're ready
for this gift.' She unravelled a gauze scarf
that shimmered with all colours of the rainbow.
'Tie this about your eyes and ears, and Spring
is all you see and hear, though to everyone else
it's invisible.' But before Grace could try,
Dame Nature threw open a door and told her
the gems in Smith's belt would be light enough
to guide her quickly underground to the wood.

'Woodwise, the great oak, expects you:
tell him from me you may ascend *The Spiral*,
or, as some call it, *Shining Stairway*.
It's the best, if not the easiest, way up
to the Rainbow and meant for those like you
who've worked faithfully to help someone else.'
Reluctantly turning to go Grace asked:
'You *will* give Don the spade?' 'Wait till you see him
using it!' said Nature as she faded from view.

Part 3

Chapters 13–18

BEYOND AND BACK

XIII

SHINING STAIRWAY

✵

At last Grace is rewarded by rising ever higher on lighter feet towards and past many enchanting wonders.

Back again in *The-Wood-That-Is-Not-There*
Grace thought a strong wind was shaking the trees.
Soon she realised it was Woodmaster Oak
waving his great arms to welcome and summon her.
Without another thought she ran to him and was lifted
high up in his branches. He pointed far away
to where the entrance gates stood firmly closed.
'No one who once enters this wood
ever returns to that gate. It's not a way out.

Look that way and you will see Don at work
with his wonderful new silver spade.'
The scene was suddenly much nearer and clearer:
it showed him digging with all his might towards
the gates, and though he could not see or hear her,
Dame Nature was teaching him to wonder
about his findings. Grace was so glad she turned
and hugged the Oak's coarse trunk, and he rumbled
his deep approval of her delight and selfless joy.

'When I lower you to the forest floor
look carefully among crisp leaves
round my feet. There's a smooth, clear crystal.'
Grace found it almost disguised by lurking toadstools.
Turning it over she read in bold, bright letters:
LET GRACE PASS AND CLIMB THE SHINING STAIRS
'Where are they?' she asked, in a rush to reach
such a quick way up to the Rainbow.
'Oh! Far from here!' boomed Woodmaster
in his Slow-Oak voice. 'But you'll get there.'
With no chance to say thanks or goodbye
she was running as fast, or faster she was sure,
than her kindly friend the swallow could fly.
Holding the crystal seemed to whirl her along,
and the quicker she went the less tired she felt.
As the sun set she plunged into dusk and dark

with only her enchanted belt to light the way,
and at sunrise she still strode on and on.

Gently then steeply her path went up and up
until she reached the top of a great peak.
The whole world seemed to lie far below
and she was higher than fair-weather clouds
that draped the earth with slow-moving shadows.
Closest and most clear, though in a strange place,
a broad rainbow spanned the entire dawn sky.
Sitting down to rest on a smooth rock
she found her wonder stone pulsed with many colours,
not just varieties of purple and white.
Whatever this meant, where was the stairway?
But just then the stone jumped from her grasp
and rolled away down the steep mountainside.
Scrambling breathlessly after she found it resting
near a broken circle of eight crystals just like
the one in her pocket. Suppose hers was meant
to fill the gap: should she place it there?
Would something important happen it she did so?

The moment the circle was complete there rose up
before her a great solid crystal door
shot through with dazzling light from behind.
It had no handle, just a small round slot
the size of the crystal that had whisked her here.
Would the door vanish if she broke the circle
and used the rock inscribed with her pass?
She had to try, and the piece fitted so well
it felt as if she'd put back a missing part.

This made two massive leaves swing open
without a creak or wobble. In the first blaze of light
she could see little, but as piping music
like the Dream Pedlar's began to echo round

she saw the stairway spiralling far up
like a giant silver corkscrew that twisted away
into the clear blue above. It made her think of
trying to follow skylarks as their song
winds them higher and higher in wide circles.

And the very idea came to life in a perfect blend
of flute and lark, as if the player had changed
his tune and tone to suit was Grace was thinking.
Then as her foot slipped on the first step,
who happened to be sitting there to greet her
but Heartsease? 'Didn't I leave you at home below
the wood?' 'I've many homes and haunts,' laughed her friend.
'But suddenly you're here!' exclaimed Grace.
'Why not? You arrived quickly, didn't you?

Sit down beside me. I will cover your feet
with supple shoes. You'll need them to climb
the crystal steps.' This new footwear flickered between
gold and silver, and Grace thought *wondershine*
must surely be at work again. But while they were fitted
she looked up the stairway. Halfway round each spiral
stood figures that looked like golden-white lilies
with half their petals opened to face upwards,
while the rest were folded down across their hearts.

Attached to the long, fair hair of each watcher
a gem danced with fire like a distant star.
Were these fragments of shooting stars that fell
and came to rest on guardians of the winding crystal?
It wasn't only Grace's thoughts that leapt to life:
these new shoes seemed to make her feet take wing.
The steps ahead looked so terribly steep
and yet she floated up. 'If only I could climb
like this forever!' she shouted back to Heartsease.

'Think about the Rainbow,' came the serious answer.
Yes: far above was the great arch of coloured lines,
goal of all her travels and long short-cuts.
But thinking back made her stop and look down
the hollow stair-well between the many spirals
she'd climbed so lightly; and suddenly it became
a dark space inside the twisting crystal steps.
She was once more in an unlit cavern
  that might never end; above a well shaft
    she would so much rather not be bundled down;
      leaving a black pool to enter a tunnel of yews;
        left to stand confused near the pond in the wood
          by a haughty water lily who'd snubbed her;
            at the shaded gate without a key or a clue;
              cut off beside the wide, sluggish river.
A fearful dream that wound time back and showed
how near she must have been to giving up her quest.
Did spirals make you turn and think of might-have-beens?

As she climbed again all those bleak moments
might never have been. Instead many steps
pictured light and dark being woven into our lives:
  wilful children whose good hearts shine in their eyes;
    a mean hoarder inspired by his gold and silver
      to brighten the hopeless days of those who need his help;
        in winter months a poor widow's son
          works at sea but the lamp she lights each night
            will surely guide him safely home to her.

Such scenes made her more light-footed and carefree.
One polished step showed her stronger and taller
with eyes brimful of wonder and ever more alert.
Her stone looked like a pure-white crystal field
dotted by tiny rainbow-tinted leaves and flowers.
The top was in sight. A graceful lily watched
each spiral but lark notes and piping faded.
My turn to sing and celebrate, thought Grace.

Violet Heartsease,
guardian loyal and true,
you blessed me with my stone
that glowed with wonders all my way,
made me younger every day,
brought me to this shining stairway.

White, tall Lilies,
watchers kind and thoughtful
who have no need for words:
petal-shrouded hearts of gold
full of secrets never told,
joys each traveller must unfold.

Winding step-way
clear-as-crystal pathway,
this is where I long to stay,
and watch my lightning slippers play.
But you lift me on my way
to where the Rainbow gleams all day.

She was utterly surprised by these words,
by their tune and her clear, sweet voice,
though all seemed true to the way she felt,
and just as she finished so did the steps.
Time and place gave no bearings: a low, red sun
lit up a grassy plane scattered with fir trees.
She turned to wave farewell to the lilies
who'd vanished along with the stairs. What was left
of that long, quick climb?...Her bright shoes!

XIV

CASTLE IN THE AIR

✵

A chapter in which Grace is nobly entertained in what you might or might not think is a moonlit never-never land.

Evening light fast fading showed Grace
she stood near a clump of dense firs
and so high above the world it looked like a map.
An orange flower-head seemed to float down
from one branch: it was an autumn helper-spirit
gathering a thousand cones to plant and tend
in high places where fir trees liked to grow.
Too busy to talk, she thought; but she looked
so lost it stopped as if expecting a question.

'Where will this path lead? Should I follow it?'
'That depends,' said the spirit, who went quiet,
then added: '*Castle-in-the-Air*, only seen
if you walk this way at dusk and wait
for half-moon-rise: it's up early tonight,
so you are lucky.' 'Can I get in?'
'Can't be sure,' said Amber Jacket breathlessly
and disappeared with his parcel of pine cones.

So she followed the sandy track that twisted through
ever taller, thicker and darker fir trees,
glad of her jewelled belt and wondershine shoes
that surrounded her steps with a cheering glow,
until at last a waxing half-moon's gleaming leaf
showed above a distant hill. It seemed to smile
in welcome, and though it had little to spare,
scattered patches of glitter across her lonely path.
To her delight they fell as luminous strips of silk
and she could lay them out in countless patterns.
And then, as if it sprang from this game,
there before her was the castle, its towers, turrets,
leaden roofs, spy-vents shining as if painted
in silver. The walls were blocks of pure moonlight
and latticed windows sparkled like precious gems.
Suppose the moon was hidden: would it be no more?
Soft, low clouds drifted about it to show

this was well and truly a castle in the air.
For a long while Grace was spellbound.

No wonder a trotting horse startled her!
Who could be riding up the fir-lined track towards her?
A pure-white steed with flowing mane and tail outshone
the moon. As Grace knew from picture histories
its rider was a knight-at-arms clad from head to foot
in silvery steel armour. His milky helmet plume
waved to and fro in time with tail and mane.
When he drew nearer she thought his suit of armour
was made of moonlight, perhaps the very same one
Round-Eyes were working at in Smith's forge,
where the fire gave it a pale blue light.
So perhaps this was Sir Cloudy Lost-Heart,
or should she call him Sir Substantial?
Round-Eye-One made him sound old, kind
but rather crazy like Alice's White Knight
in *Through the Looking-Glass*. But off came
the helmet to reveal piercing, lively eyes
and golden hair thick and well-groomed.

At first he said nothing, noticed her belt and knew
she'd been to the forge, could tell from her shoes
she must have ascended the shining spiral stairs.
Though her left hand was firmly clenched round
her wonder stone, he saw its glow and sensed its power.
Grace was also still and quiet, which gave her time
to wonder why a gold chain that hung from his neck
bore a *wooden* heart, though finely painted with
many rainbow-coloured patterns and devices.

Why wasn't it precious gold and silver if he lived
in that grand palace? Such were her thoughts
when the young knight bowed politely:
'Young lady, I wish you a good evening.

May I ask your name and if you're bound for
my castle?' (*Oh dear!* She thought. Fancy thinking
he'd be a dear, old well-meaning White Knight,
all nonsense and silly games!) 'I'm called Grace,'
she said gravely: 'I'd like to come and visit your castle.'

'Then we'll go together,' said he. 'I'm now called
Sir Cloudy Lost-Heart, though many still address me
as Sir Substantial Nebule. You can overlook that!'
'I hoped to meet you,' answered Grace. 'I imagined
you would be as ancient as Smith or Woodwise.'
Sir Cloudy laughed like distant festive bells
pealing through a clear, sharp moonlit night.
'I shall never grow old because I've wandered
on the far side of the Rainbow, where I received
the blessing of a young heart open to wonder.'
'I long to go there,' said Grace, hoping for
for some guidance and advice. His reply

was not really what she wanted to hear.
'We're bound to meet there. I've a secret route
from my castle to the Rainbow, which is only
open to those who've first found their own way there.'
His smile said: *Sorry: that's how it must be!*
She smiled back. And they were glad to have met.

Sir Cloudy invited her to mount behind his saddle.
Two youngsters were no weight for his horse.
So on they cantered towards the stately castle,
and the closer they came the clearer shone the moonlight
on ever loftier towers and ornamental battlements
circled by a moat filled with liquid moonshine
from a glassy lake that stretched into the night.
The portcullis was locked, the drawbridge up,
but at one blast from his silver horn
servants in blue and silver uniform winched up
the spiked grill and wound down the plank bridge
without a creak or groan. These agile men
looked like castle attendants but were guardian spirits
who looked after the knight. They showed no surprise
at Grace's arrival, though visitors were rare:
they knew without being told her gift
for wonder and how she'd journeyed to come this far.
Out of respect they touched their shining caps
that matched the castle's roof cones. Two helped her
dismount before Sir Cloudy took her right hand
and courteously led her into his spacious hallway.
What a vast and elaborate dwelling for two
youngsters like the knight and his wide-eyed guest!
They sat on high-backed moonlight chairs close to
high latticed windows, their hundreds of diamond shapes
alight with ever-changing colours. Time to show
each other and admire their precious belongings.
He explained in detail how Smith and his dwarves
forged and hinged his armour to make it feel light

as a suit of clothes yet fend off every weapon
or swiftest arrow if he had to undertake
distant and dangerous quests. Knowing a little about
knightly feats of arms Grace asked politely
why he carried no mace, lance, sword or shield,
a question that seemed greatly to puzzle him at first!

'Weapons are for attack or to defend oneself.
The first I never engage in; and my armour
is so strong and dazzling I don't need a shield.'
Her turn to be puzzled, and she wondered
what kind of quests he had to follow. Instead
she told him all about her various adventures.
He listened intently and said how much like
his own they were but his eyes kept returning
to and dwelling on her jewel-flecked belt.

He also began to look wistful, even downcast.
'I've lost my greatest treasure.' 'I'm so very sorry,'
said Grace. 'Tell me what it is. Perhaps there's a way
we can find it.' She knew what it would be like
to lose her wonder stone. 'It's my moonstone heart,'
said Sir Cloudy with a sigh. 'That's why I wear
a wooden one. I have to, you see. My crest contains
a heart, and I must not leave here without
one hanging from my neck. My knighthood's at stake.'

'Where did you lose this heart?' 'I fear it's been stolen.
I fell asleep in moonlight when I should always
be wide awake. It had vanished by dawn.
Grace, never fall asleep where you shouldn't.
It serves me right that I'll have to make do
with this wooden imitation.' His friend felt
more hopeful. 'What if some guardian spirits
have hidden it to make you take more care?'
He was not convinced and looked rather hurt.

'I'll never see it again,' he said gloomily.
He felt in need of sympathy not advice!
'But I'll help you search for it,' insisted Grace,
jumping from her seat. 'It's surely somewhere
in the castle rooms you use most often.'
She searched every corner of the great hall,
some thick with dust (even in this airy palace!)
She shook cushions, crept under tables and cabinets,
scoured window seats and the chests below them.

At last only the wide, high fireplace flickering
with moonshine flames had escaped her busy eyes.
Then she thought of the gauze scarf, Clover's gift,
unravelled it from a pocket and wrapped it round
her eyes and ears. Just as she had been told
spring birds sang, the air was filled with the scent
of primrose, hyacinth and bluebell. Outshining
the bejewelled windows and beyond the moat
orchards were white with cherry, pear and apple blossom.

But more amazing still, high above her head
hanging over the hearth on its slender chain
glowed a moonstone heart, so intricately worked
countless stars seemed to gleam in one heart shape.
Grace was taller and stronger since she'd climbed the stairway
and found it easy to reach up and grasp the treasure.
Then she ran across the hall and threw it round
Sir Cloudy's neck, which delighted him so much
he danced her round and round the polished floor until
they were out of breath with movement and laughter.
'I thought I'd looked everywhere. Where did you
light upon it? There's more to you than meets the eye!'
Whether or not the moonlight made her mischievous
Grace shook her finger and said playfully:
'That's my secret, Sir Cloudy Lost-Heart.
Oh, and will you think of changing your title now?'

This rather pleased him, and what did it matter
how his heart was found? It hung where it belonged.

'Well I'm much indebted to you, dear Grace.'
He bowed, took and kissed her hand respectfully.
'The change you suggest makes good sense
but every knight must keep his family nickname.
'Now it's time to have our supper served, and then
I must bid you farewell, for no one may stay
overnight in the *Castle-in-the-Air*
till he or she has crossed the rainbow bridge and found
what lies beyond. The entire building
would fade away around you. You might even
grow old inside your head and have no gift for wonder.
But once you've reached the rainbow realm I'll be there
and escort you back to be my honoured guest.'
A high, soft note on his horn summoned
waiters in blue and silver uniforms. They laid
the table with silver forks, spoons and crystal goblets,
and many small dishes of fresh and dried fruits,
seeds, nuts, forest mushrooms and fresh-baked rolls.

The cook, an inquisitive, clever spirit
disguised in bleached-white kitchen uniform
peeped in to see who the guest might be,
and quickly sent in a plate of little cakes
flavoured with almonds and covered in moonbow-tinted icing.
She sensed the journey Grace had made and this was
a treat to reward her for all those testing times.
It added colour and sweetness to a feast
even finer than the one prepared by Heartsease
to welcome her back. The knight and his guest
drank each other's health in best moonshine wine
that set you ever so lightly adrift on silver wings.
When they'd finished, Sir Cloudy summoned a boat
by blowing a special note on his horn.

It was to carry his visitor in comfort gently
along the moonshine moat on to Long Lake
and out into River Daylight, an untroubled
waterway from airy castle to rainbow realms.

While attendants made ready and lowered the boat,
Grace was led down narrow paved stairs
to a round door that opened as if it knew
its master. He told her to look inside.
It was his direct secret way to the Rainbow
and the array of pure colours left her dazzled
and dazed for a moment. 'You'll return this way,'
said the knight before the entrance shut tight
as if to say: 'Wait!' Another square door
looked like studded moon-silver armour.
It lead to a closet full of cabinets
containing priceless jewels. He opened a drawer,
took something out and hung it round her neck.
It was the garland she'd seen in Smith's deft fingers:
silver celandines, buttercups and primroses,
so lightly-textured they rustled like wind-blown leaves.
'Smith's cleverly crafted chaplet feels meant
for you, and I'm honoured to make a gift of it.'

'Is this for me to wear?' Grace was astonished.
'I have many items brighter and more precious
but I am most attached to this, which is why
I would like it to be yours. The enchanted flowers
restore strength. They will assist your passage to
the Rainbow garden. But now I must warn you firmly:
beware of a Menace that haunts the Fields of Plenty.
It lies in wait among the crops that ripen beside
the broad River Daylight, and will be after
this necklace, hoping its powers can be used to blunt
and twist the gifts of wonder that have brought
wanderers like you so near their many-coloured goal.'

'What does this menace look like?' asked Grace.
'And how does it behave?' After all this time,
she thought, I'm in sight of the Rainbow realms
and something is waiting to ruin my chances.
'The Menace takes on many guises on to suit
its victim but charm is its main weapon.

'Its favourite trick,' added the knight, 'is to make
you fall asleep just when you shouldn't.
Perhaps that's how I lost my heart of gold.
But be sure to walk through the Fields of Plenty
with confidence. Fear and doubt make it easier
for the Menace to trap you in its wiles.'
Just then a servant announced that the boat
was afloat and ready, and they climbed down
to a jetty built inside the castle walls
behind iron gates that opened into the moat.
'Farewell, my dear young lady and my friend
in the boundless realms of open-minded wonder.'
Heartfelt but formal words that just concealed
a note of sadness in the young knight's voice.
'We'll meet again,' he added. 'Yes, safely
beyond the Rainbow arch, if only I pass through
those fields,' said Grace as bravely as she could.
Sir Cloudy gently lifted her right hand and kissed it.

Later she noticed this kiss had left behind
a slowly-fading moonstone heart. Time now to step into
the polished boat and sit on soft blue cushions
while a uniformed boatman prepared and fixed
silver-banded-and-bladed oars and rowed almost
without splash or ripple round the moonshine moat
and through a silver-doored sluice on to the lake's
moonlit sheet, so still and clear it felt as if
they were skimming across liquid glass.

And as Grace drifted away and faded into
the unknown, Sir Cloudy and all his servant spirits
stood together on the airy castle's highest walls
and sang a safe-voyage part song, in simple words
but complicated harmonies which pleased the knight.

Lady Grace,
float still, safe and sound,
float on your moonlit way,
float round moat and over long lake,
float into the River of Day
where larks chant daylong tirra-lirra.

Boatman, serve your lady
with boat strong-ribbed and silver-bound,
softly ply and feather oars
to cut your watery way,
skim moat, glide over long lake
till you part the River of Day
where dawn larks rise with tirra-lirra.

XV

MENACE

✵

Even so near to her goal darkness and destruction linger. Grace makes a serious mistake but refuses to give in, befriends a lost soul and is encouraged by an all-seeing winged guide.

Grace sat in the stern of the boat and turned
from time to time to watch the castle fade away
in moonlit mist. She let her hand wash along
in moonshine water and the moonbeams trickled down
and swirled on the surface like playful fish.
The rower who faced her was quiet and intent
on making headway, and soon his endless wheeling
strokes became a pendulum that lulled her to sleep.
She woke to find the lake had narrowed into
a reedy channel, and the ferryman muttered grimly:
'Soon be at the wide river, swift and strong,
so take good hold till we're well astride
its broad, bucking back.' But Grace enjoyed
the sudden helter-skelter, and the little boat,
much cheerier than its master, leapt along
like a dog let off its leash. What worried her
was that Menace. Would it appear among the waving
ripe corn that skirted the river's right bank?

The warm, peaceful scene tempted her to wonder
if Sir Cloudy made too much of this threat.
Her stone was plain mauve, a perfect amethyst
keeping its counsel! Ahead Rainbow Arch spanned
the horizon and a low dawn sun.
They set the river ablaze with a mass of colours.
Bright, lively River of Day, thought Grace.
Carry me past my troubles to the Rainbow.
But in a calm inlet there stood a wooden pier.

Mooring the boat and helping Grace to alight
the oarsman was at last quite talkative:
'Mind out for the Menace. Some call it
Poppy Pest. See its red flags waving
where they will, up to no good in the corn?
Be quick about getting to the Rainbow garden.'
'Thank you for your work and advice,' she answered.

✤ Menace ✤

'How will you row into that current?'
'I've ways!' His cunning look was nearly a smile!

They shook hands and off he rowed, keeping
to the far bank, while Grace followed a path
that wound slowly upwards through the tall wheat.
Her blue and silver waterman felt like
a last contact with the enchanting castle
so she turned to wave goodbye only to find
no sign of a boat on the wide river,
which made her feel almost as lonely as
when her basket reached the bottom of the well.

The ears of wheat whispered and nodded in the breeze,
but they seemed far too busy to notice her.
Among them, as the tight-lipped boatman said,
floated tall, floppy red poppies making the most
of their brief time in flower, too proud
surely to bother with some meddling menace.
How could she lose this precious flower necklace
that jingled like a tiny tambourine and danced
with sunlight round her neck? It was hers for ever.

Then suddenly she found herself in
a round open space overlooked by poppies
who seemed to be watching an invisible show.
It looked so comfortable, lined with old straw
matted together by creeping corn-cockle.
If only she could lie and rest for a minute!
When she lay down and stretched out it felt
like a bed made for weary noonday walkers,
and she closed her eyes to stop the sun staring .

At once some poppy gazers turned aside
and signalled to something or someone hidden away
in the crops. There was a loud rustle and trampling

of corn stalks which Grace missed, for the poppies
were filling the air about her with a soft-toned song
that made it feel quite safe and sensible to fall asleep.

We'll shade your eyes from sun's hot reach
sleepy-headed wonder-weary Grace.
Rest safely while we stand on watch
and send a cooling breeze across your face.
Corn hugs and hides no snugger place
with soft brown earth to cushion you.
Sleep soundly dreamy-headed Grace
until our petals brush on you
when the moon is riding high and bright
and spirits bid you join their nightly dance,
linger long in feast and talk till light
returns and sends you on to take your chance.

Grace had almost given in and fallen asleep
when Sir Cloudy's urgent words came back:
Never fall asleep where you shouldn't. Was this
the wrong place? It felt so inviting!
She sat up straight and made her herself look around,
which alarmed the poppies who tightened their petals
in disappointment; but once those charming sleepy spells
begin, waves of drowsiness roll in
however hard you fight them, and when Grace started
to nod like a foolish wilting noonday poppy,
there was another rustling upheaval in the corn,
and she heard a voice close to her ears.
'Pleased to meet you,' it said most cordially.
'Such a warm day! Grace might like a sleep.'
'Strange! Someone I've never set eyes on
seems to know me. Who can it be?'
By now she'd almost forgotten where she was
and for all she knew this might be a dream.

✤ Menace ✤

The speaker was a tubby little man, dressed
in a tight, creased earth-brown suit
under a broad poppy-red hat. Ugly,
and too red in the face, thought Grace,
but worse when he screwed it up in a smirk.
Still he seemed to want to be of service
so she tried hard not to think about his looks.
It couldn't be Mister Menace. Would he
speak in such a gentle, well-meaning way?

Had the chanting poppies stopped her thinking clearly?
And what about the knight's clear warning?
The menace has many guises and uses charm
to trick its victims. 'Ye-es, I *am* so-oh tired!'
agreed Grace with a yawn and no *excuse-me.*
'Time for a tune,' said the little round man
as if this might help, and out of his pocket came
various bits of flute he quickly screwed together.
But blowing soon made him look ready to burst.

His face glowed like a live, hot coal
and it was all she could do not to laugh.
'Ah well, expect you're not at all musical,'
said her companion, offended and out of breath.
'I liked the Dream Pedlar's piping,' said Grace
with another wide yawn, 'but please excuse me,
I'm far too tired to listen to anything.'
Then turning to one side she fell fast asleep
and slept long and deeply till mid afternoon.

Where on earth was she? The poppies around her
were busy being themselves and looked
as if they'd never had anything to say.
As for her new friend he'd vanished into
thin air, or *fat*, thought Grace with disgust,
suddenly needing to check on her gifts.

Gold and silver slippers glittered on her feet,
Smith's bejewelled belt clasped her waist,
Wonder Stone sat firmly in her left palm.

But where was the knight's flower necklace?
Gone! Stolen, of course, by the smiling Menace.
O Grace you fell asleep in the wrong place!
How will you enter the Rainbow garden now?
Will your Rainbow quest take even longer?
She wept tears of anger at her foolishness
and wanted to shake that devious little thief.
But Grace had a brave heart and wouldn't admit
defeat. Time to think hard, she decided.

'When did I get anywhere by crying?'
she asked herself aloud. 'We'll just find
the menace, collar him and claim back the chain.'
(That was how her uncle spoke when someone
at last exhausted even his patience!)
She left her fatal refuge without a glance at
the poppies and never noticed their mocking laughter,
so pleased were they with their trickery.
Running back downhill she hoped to catch the menace
once he was out of the corn. But he never left it
even during harvest or when fields were ploughed and sown
for he lived below ground with his mother,
an ancient hag who taught him malice and deceit.
And Grace soon returned to the Daylight River
which no longer danced with light or hurried
with delight at being alive. Its sluggish surface
was filmed with oil, and rotting rubbish lined its banks.
She clasped her stone in wonder: it looked blank and pale.

Rows of barges full of cargo were tied up
or being towed by rattling steam tug boats
whose skippers looked bored and tired. And beyond

rose up lines of squat houses fanning out
like spokes in a wheel from a massive factory.
Its rows of giant smoking chimneys filled the skyline.
The air almost tasted of soot and stagnant water.
Such places were nothing new to Grace, but why
had one sprouted up here as if to add to
her troubled feelings? Was it yet another trick
played by the menace to sidetrack her from
the Rainbow quest? But just then she noticed
an old man leaning on the wire fence
that cordoned off the river as if it were a railway.
He looked for all the world like a grown-up Don,
downcast too, as well as hopeless and worn-out.
She felt sorry for him, forgot her own worries,
and by way of a friendly greeting smiled warmly.

He just shook his head. 'Can't seem to smile,'
he grunted. 'Don't even know how to laugh,
or maybe there's nothing here to amuse me.'
'That sounds dreadful. When you were younger
you must have laughed.' 'Now I've no reason to.'
He spoke in a gloomy drawl as if finding words
was too much. How could she cheer him up?
She couldn't give him her stone or enchanted belt,
and another silver spade was quite impossible.
Then she thought of Clover's gift, the gauze scarf
tucked away since she used it in the castle.
'Would you like to see and hear spring whenever
you want?' 'That might well cheer me up,' he said.
'I'd feel like a boy on a country outing,
or at least remember how it used to be.'
'Tie this round your eyes and ears.' She helped him,
pitying his thin, grimy hair and the way
his scraggy neck bent forward from stooping shoulders.

He laughed happily and stood almost upright.
'There are fruit tree orchards in blossom all round
those town houses. The muddy bank's turned green;
daisies and buttercups have sprung up everywhere.
Birds are singing in the lacy-white blackthorn hedges.
Pity I never learned to recognize their songs.
Some restless bird is perched on that signpost
by the field. Seems to want you to notice it!'
'My friend the swallow! I didn't see a post there.
He may want me to go back the way I came.
Keep the scarf and refresh yourself with spring
when days feel dark and the world weighs you down.'
Cheering up the old man had given Grace
a way with words and made her more hopeful.
Yes: swallow was there, waiting anxiously!
'I'm ready to go south again but before
I join my family and friends in autumn flight
I must tell you what's happened to your necklace.'

'Dear swallow! Surprising me with help again!'
'I'll be away all winter and when I'm gone
I can do nothing, so try to stay awake!'
He wasn't going to overlook her silly mistake.
This was the one time when swallows perched
and chattered, and he had a lot more to say.
'You will reach the Rainbow, and for a while
your troubles will be over.' '*And* my travels!'
She sighed with regret. 'Adventures don't end
beyond a rainbow quest. Now about that necklace.
Master Menace dwells below the wheat fields
with his cunning, twisted old hag of a mother.
He's long been after a powerful chainlet. Why
I can't tell, but certainly to no good end.
He's so careless, lazy and fond of sleep

from dusk till dawn, he leaves mother to keep
watch, while she stirs and stirs some vile mixture
in a great fire-heated pan and seldom looks up.'

'What's in the pan?' asked Grace. 'A potent, deadly
sleeping draught made from berries of woody nightshade,
poppy seed and foxglove root. Don't touch it!
This is what you *must* do. Wait till nightfall
when poppies fall asleep and can no longer warn
the menace. It's only the hag who never sleeps.
Creep along till you see among the corn
the shadowy outline of three phantom elms
with red-tinged smoke rising between them. By day
they cannot be seen. Below the roots lies a cave
where the menace sleeps with your necklace hanging
above his head. Creep in softly and snatch it
while the mother's busy with her brew.' 'Suppose she sees me?'
'There's a pot of dust mixed with ash and grit
kept to throw at unwanted callers. Make sure
you get there first and throw a handful at her.'
'I couldn't do that!' Grace objected strongly.
'It just weakens her for a moment,' said the swallow.

'Did you see the menace steal my flower necklace?'
she asked. 'Yes: then followed him and spotted his den.
Since then I've talked to many insects and birds.
I was born curious. Some say I'm nosey!
Now I must fly fast to catch the others.'
'Goodbye, I'll look out for you next spring.'
In seconds he was out of sight, or had he vanished
along with the old man and smoke-filled town?
No time to dwell on that. It was dusk
and Grace stole quietly along the wheat-field path
where poppies had bent their heads in sleep.
Her belt lit the way, though she kept brushing against
corn stalks... She stopped and held her breath in case

someone had heard. Soon she spotted the smoking trees,
tufts of black night crouched on pale fields,
and as she drew nearer saw a red glow
filling a round hole. Must she venture below
ground yet again to finish her journey?

She crept down jagged steps of root and rock
into an earth-walled, filthy cavern that served as kitchen,
living and sleeping room. The fat little menace
was spread out fast asleep on mat-covered logs,
still in his close-fitting suit, poppy hat
crammed over his red face and loud snores.
His mother stirred her foul-smelling pan on
a roaring fire whose smoke escaped through charred roots
into the trees above. Her face was lined and leathery,
her hair like long strands of matted thistle-down,
her bulging nose, thought Grace, must be made of
several prize horse-chestnuts stuck together.
She was draped in a thick black cloak
dotted with hundreds of red poppy heads.
And there beside her stood a great urn of dust.
Luckily she hadn't noticed her visitor,
so Grace was free to look around, and *there*, sparkling
in firelight, was the necklace she longed to recover.

It was stuck on ivy that had strayed down
in search of light. Stretching up she seized the leaves
and pulled off her gift, or did it leap
gladly into her hand? But skirting round
the slumped and snoring menace she tripped on
his boots and fell into a pile of dry sticks.
He just snorted, turned away and slept on.
The hag shot round and leapt at the girl
who was up in a flash, darting and dodging round
the crowded clutter and that log-like menace
the mother daren't wake for fear of his temper.

✣ Menace ✣

Then her cloak stuck fast on an upturned stool
so Grace took handful after handful of dust
to hurl at the harpy who spat and cursed,
rubbed her stinging eyes and coughed till she choked.
Time to scramble back to the now moonlit fields;
but she mustn't get lost in the corn
which was where the evil pair wielded power.

She soon found the path and ran as hard as she could
till it dipped into a lane between tall hedges.
Their flowers did not shine moonlit white and silver
but rainbow colours, and when she clipped her necklace on
it made rainbow spinning wheels. The promised garden
must be near. And the gently-scented track led to
a willow-woven gate set in a prickly hedge
laden with rainbow berries. Daylight blazed through
the barrier as if she stood in a moonlit tunnel.

XVI

RAINBOW GARDEN

✵

Where Grace sees, hears and smells so much that reflects more perfectly what she recalls from home or elsewhere on her journey. Even here there's a misfit she feels bound to care for.

Grace felt sure this must be the gateway
into Rainbow Garden. She glanced at Wonder Stone
and found it full of rainbow-coloured stripes
on a pearl-white background. Would wondering open
this tightly-woven barrier? Perhaps! Three beetles
on watch sensed a presence in the dark
beyond their bright realms, and knew it was Grace,
for they had helped build a rainbow bridge across
the broad sluggish river to reach another gate.

So long ago and far off to her. To them
only hours before and a quick flight away
to offer skills the kindly guardians required.
They noticed she was wearing Sir Cloudy's necklace,
and a quick wave of the leader's antlers
made the gate spring noiselessly apart as if
the tall hedge had swallowed it. 'Welcome Grace:
we've been expecting you. Come and discover
life-giving wonders and hear a tale or two.'

It was enjoyment enough to be here at last.
'The menace has tormented and delayed me,' she said,
in case she had kept her friends waiting.
The beetles gave each other a knowing look and nod.
'Mother and son love beetle stew, and she
hunts for her prey in the ripening corn
where our tribe are at work protecting the plants.
She sprinkles them with drops of her brew
and once they are asleep what can they do?

'But never mind that now. You can wander
wherever you like, quickly or slowly.
Those like you who've journeyed this far
need never be in any one place
at a certain time. Whatever you choose
to stop and think about is meant for you.'

Which only told Grace how she felt:
light-footed and delighted to be free from
the thought of having to be somewhere else.

She danced along a shorn carpet of camomile
that wound through endless clumps of primrose,
cowslip and multi-coloured oxlip. Each footfall
set off a sharp sweetness that blended so perfectly
with the heady spring flowers, she must be afloat
on gentle waves of green, red and yellow scent.
She then passed under a holly-hedge arch
into a round enclosure bathed in warm sunlight,
ripening berries on every kind of fruit bush
that came to mind. How she surprised herself
by just drinking in all these shapes and colours!
No rush to look for what was ripe and ready
to pick and eat! Then past the far archway rose
a grove of tall cedars shading dew-cooled grass
laced with all her favourite bulbs in full flower.
She walked among them to savour what seemed like
chatter and laughter as if she'd stumbled on
a party held to celebrate unending spring.

Grace began to feel that in this garden
you might see, smell, hear, touch or taste
without quite knowing which you were doing.
She trod carefully not to spoil their happiness
but every plant swerved aside to let her pass,
so even the tiniest snowdrop, crocus or aconite
was quite safe from her glittering stairway shoes,
which carried her in the space of a few breaths
into a maze of flowering shrubs and small trees.

Bees hummed contentedly among catkin-flowers
of her favourite hazels, willows, alders and birches.
Along the branches and around their feet

all the song birds she liked to watch and hear
were busy feeding, trying out their tunes and trills,
running here and there or soaring in elaborate flight
for sheer joy at being alive and together.
It reminded Grace of when she left the dark wood
and found slender song-filled trees beside a stream.

There she was passing by and looking out for
a hard climb ahead. *Here* it was her moment
and everything seemed to wait and be pleased
to embrace and delight her. And as if
to answer thoughts of rocky paths that twisted
into empty skylines, a tall, slim palace appeared
in the distance. It was made from many-coloured
pillars of light, and quite round, with one row of round
windows under its one vast dazzling roof cone.

Now she was walking lightly towards it
across an open plane like a vast carpet
woven with close-packed clumps of living flowers.
Though moving forward she was in the hub
of a turning wheel divided by invisible
spokes into nine ever-exchanging colours.
She recognised the nine plants that dressed those guardians
who'd brought her gifts. But they kept slipping into
rainbow-tinted *rose-carnation-dahlia* shapes.
For a moment their leaves were black, their stalks white
but they too were passing through every colour
along with the bees and insects that worked among them.
On her long journey Grace had never felt
so enthralled, which made her stone pulse
and match the whirling scene in perfect miniature.
The palace looked closer, standing at the summit
of the rainbow arch, and she could see how
rays from its pillars played across the plane.

All these colours and changing shapes swirled about her
as if she'd walked into her own kaleidoscope,
and there she might have stood for many an hour had not
a passing brimstone-yellow butterfly doubled back,
circled round and round and caught her attention.
'Whose is that palace?' she asked, and realised
this was another friend who'd helped suspend
a bridge across that monstrous, lazy river
by adding tightly-locked swathes of light. 'Ah, Grace!
I flew back in case it was you. And it is!
Let me welcome you, as will the Colour Guardians
who are now at home among those radiant pillars.
You have met them. Here they take on new splendour.
Your one path across the rainbow is through that one
first door into the one high, round hall
where you will consult with them before leaving
by the one far door to make your happy way
down the beaming arch and on into your future.'

'Thank you! But what should I call you?'
'Names don't matter to us. *Butterfly* will do.'
Grace wondered and worried a little about what
awaited her beyond the rainbow and its palace.
'I feel there can be no finer place than this.'
Her guide knew what lay behind these words:
'You'll be surprised by what's in store for you
across the rainbow. So much to unfold!
A journey begun this well never ends.'

Though she was too polite to say so, Grace felt
this made sense and nonsense all at once.
But after these parting words her friend had flapped
away into the shimmering distance, and she wandered down
a little dell that cut through the rainbow plane
and felt like a restful place for plants and shrubs
that liked each other's company. In long grass beside

a mossy bank ox-eye daisies grew in clusters.
Almost to herself she said: 'How pleasant
to sit and rest beside so many cheerful ox-eyes.
Too often you're scattered over stony plough-land.'
'Well, well!' said a tall, strong plant.
'We also like to be called moon-daisies.
Unlike most of our ancient family
we don't close up after dark,
and we're said to like the moon's borrowed light.'
'But here,' said Grace, 'there's always light and warmth
so you must feel quite content and trouble-free.'

All these colours and changing shapes swirled about her as if she'd walked into her own kaleidoscope…

Then she heard a soft sobbing from somewhere
among the moon-daisies, though they all seemed
to be smiling, but peering closer she noticed
one small plant had folded its petals and moved
from side to side as if shaken by a breeze
the others didn't feel, and neither could Grace.
So she knelt down and whispered: 'What troubles you
in this bright, carefree place?' How tender
are this girl's eyes, thought the drooping daisy,
and said: 'Without my friend the sunflower I'm lost
and lonely, even though I'm glad to grow beside
my own kith and kin.' 'Where is your friend?'
asked Grace kindly, for she was sure nothing alive
should be unhappy in the Rainbow Garden.
'I'm afraid I don't know,' came the answer
in a tearful tone, but the flower thought
it time to show what lay behind her tears,
so she told a rather formal tale like this.

A moon-daisy lived in a meadow
near a hedge too high to see across.
Beyond it grew a well-planted garden
and one tall sunflower saw the daisy
waving gently in the wandering breeze,
pearl-white smile on a slender stem,
and she looked back and loved his splendour.
'Let nothing part us and we'll live
in one of Nature's nurseries under hill.'

Happy together, this was their hope,
until the householders had to move,
the sunflower was taken to a town-yard
and the meadow ploughed for greater profit.
So watchful spirits seeing how she wilted
revived the daisy as a rainbow moonflower
to dwell in light among her lively family.

But even here how could she be happy
when nothing bright blazed like her friend?

Grace could not help thinking about her friendship
with Sir Cloudy and how his last kiss left
a slowly fading moonstone heart on her hand.
Would he be as good as his word and meet her
beyond the Rainbow? And while she wandered among
these dreams and memories three bumble bees, striped
black, gold and red buzzed round and round
until they came to rest on three moon-daisies,
close enough for her to tell they'd once worked
in that party summoned by the Dream Piper,
making safe the bridge's beetle-back way
with pollen and honey. 'Friends! Three of the nine who came
to help me. So far from where I watched you work.'
'Yes' answered one, sizzling and busy-sounding.
'Distance never daunts us. If you'd like to send
one of us afar we're ready to assist.'
'This heart-broken daisy longs to live beside
her long-lost sunflower friend,' said Grace, and asked:
'Couldn't you find a way to carry him here?'

One of the bees answered slowly and frankly.
'He'd be a great weight. And it's not
yet time for him to live in this place.
But I will go and see what can be done.'
Away it flew and gave Grace something hopeful
to tell the pale-leaved daisy. A long flight
and longer search, you would have thought,
but whether or not time and distance counted little,
the bee was soon back and settled on Grace's hand
looking pleased, purposeful and as fresh
as if it had flown from one flower to another.
'I found the sunflower. He's lonely, too,
growing in a pot. The back-street yard

sees so little sun his quest for light makes him
look stretched and thin. I could carry
the moon-daisy's heart and plant it beside him
to flourish next spring. But what a dim corner
for her after bathing in perpetual light!'

'The sunflower will be beside her,' said Grace.
'Then I will offer to take her,' replied the bee,
who'd not told the sunflower what was planned
for fear of disappointing him, and now buzzed
towards the daisy who lit up with sudden hope.
'Your friend's home is a pot surrounded
by walls. Do you still want to join him?'
'Why should I mind if he's nearby?'
So the bee took her soft yellow heart
and made two farewell circles round Grace.
Later she learnt how the sunflower had looked
brighter and stronger once the bee had planted
the lively little heart in rich earth next to
his stem, for now they'd grow so much closer
than that summer when a hedge divided them.
A success the bee had celebrated
by making up a song as it flew back
and very much wanted Grace to listen to.

A small bumble-bee had too big a heart
to let the best of friends live far apart.

He left the garden blessed with light of day
and took the mournful daisy all the way

to lay her longing heart gently down
and grow beside the sunflower in a smoky town.

Opening their summer buds they'll meet
each other's smile and feel complete.

Grace praised the song, though she much preferred
moon-daisy's simple little tale, and really her mind
kept wandering back to Sir Cloudy and whether she might
meet him once she'd passed through the palace and down
the far side. And hadn't this flower story
and rescue journey become yet another long
way round? What Aunt Miriam called a sidetrack!
She might have guessed the Rainbow Garden would not
open a quick way towards reaching her goal,
about which the butterfly had left her puzzled.

Though impatient to get on, she knew full well
she could not have ignored the mournful moon-daisy
any more than Downcast Don's need for help.
So after saying a warm, kind goodbye to the bee
she rejoined the path through revolving gardens
towards the Rainbow Palace and quickly reached
broad mother-of-pearl steps that flowed up
the great bow curve and seemed to go on for ever,
for at their foot the palace was out of sight.

XVII

RAINBOW PALACE

✵

A simpler place than you might expect but one to wonder at. Colours have much to say, as do the guardians, when Grace is invited to see many things in a new light, both close-to and from afar.

The steps felt at once soft and solid
as they flashed through every rainbow colour
and turned gold when Grace's slippers touched them.
Perhaps it was the way hundreds of shades melted
and merged that made her feel the higher she climbed
the more blocks rose up ahead, making her wonder
so much her stone grew heavier and heavier
though no larger. But she reached the great door
just when the weight became unbearable.

Then the gem became light as air and glowed
with such depth she thought her palm had turned violet.
More amazing was what she saw when looking back.
No steps, but sloping steeply away and down
into misty fathomless space an ever-changing band
of many-coloured rays, and the glorious gardens
she'd longed for and loved were nowhere to be seen.
'That's half the rainbow. Now for the palace
that flickers so much I wonder how steady it is.'

A thought that made the shining door disappear
into its archway, inviting Grace to enter
a lofty round hall whose walls looked like marble,
white but laced with purple strands. Half way up
and evenly spaced were nine huge round windows,
eight of separate rainbow colours, one purest white.
Opposite stood the door she'd leave by
to descend the rainbow. In this towering vault
not even a faint echo disturbed her wonder.

For a while she was taken up with how
colour from each window divided the floor into
nine sectors just like the revolving garden.
And in the centre they all blended and whirled
clockwise in a fiery wheel that drew her
to look more closely, but without realising

she walked straight through it only to feel
the hall spin like a merry-go-round as if
it was preparing to show her so much more.

Then she noticed figures in flowing robes who sat
on a high dais that ran round the wall
so they could look through the window that matched
the colour they wore. Surely these must be guardians,
and, as the Brimstone Butterfly had said,
in an even more splendid guise than the moment
they appeared with gifts before her travels began.
Even then they formed a kind of rainbow,
as Heartsease hinted before she merged with morning light.

So caring for plants and people blessed with wonder
were only some of their tasks and part of their power.
Here they worked at looms placed below
their windows, drawing thread from round bales
that glistened with rainbow colours. Some wove
ever-changing sunset or sunrise patterns.
The guardian she'd seen as Sunflower made
light beams and shed them in glittering heaps.
Heartsease spun tapestries of evening scenes.

As busy as Primers, Painters and Protectors
she'd seen and heard in Nature's under-hill halls,
they sang softly to the rhythm of their work.
Red, blue, violet, green,
crimson glow, purple sheen,
        into thoughts we're weaving.
Sunrise stormy warning red,
sunset intricately spread,
        into dreams we're making.
Colours in-between and rare,
that waver as you stare,
        from pot of gold we're mingling.

✣ Rainbow ✣

O rainbow arch of rays
we sing your praise
in woven work unceasing.

The song mentioned something Grace had not noticed.
A wide white crystal pot slowly turned
in the middle of the whirling fiery wheel.

Though the guardians drew on its riches,
it remained full to the brim with the gold
you see in slowly-fading summer sunsets.
Here just under the rainbow crown was stored
a treasury of sunbeams as they fell.
Not some fabled pot at the rainbow foot
that rewards its finder with precious metal
and undreamed-of worldly wealth, but one filled
with a kind of 'wondershine', and more priceless.

Without knowing why, Grace was most drawn
to the night-robed guardian who had appeared
as wood-shaded Bell and offered the gift of seeing
far beyond and deeply within what meets the eye.
She sat before her round dark-blue window weaving
moonbeams from her loom and turned to beckon
their visitor up spiral steps to the dais,
a hint of moonlight in her deep-blue eyes
and shimmering through the folds of her midnight gown.

'Here you are Grace at long last, your journey
nearly over. And now you'll be forever young
in mind and heart. To celebrate your wonder gift
would you like to place your gemstone on my loom?
Then I'll thread its moods and patterns into
sunset and moonrise so elaborate
all who see them will pause for thought.'
Grace could think of no better way to part
with her long-held, faithful companion.

'Once you leave here and walk down the bow
and beyond, you'll no longer need this stone.
Now take a look through my window.'
First under a perfect sun-filled blue sky
there was a long winding green path that wove
its way through places full of life and growth
that she'd passed on her travels, even the wild
unwelcoming wood she'd had to explore.
The track wound up ever-higher hills and peaks
then faded away below the shining spiral,
when the sky turned indigo blue, and moonlight
painted a pale landscape. The pathway turned silver,
and might have been stream or track but now it coiled
round in ever smaller loops till it reached
a silvery-towered, moated castle. And from it
rode a cavalcade of horsemen with banners
and plumed helmets, their heralds in blue and silver
blowing bugles to announce a great occasion.

Grace felt this meant Sir Cloudy had set out
to meet her again as he had promised;
but before she could ask about this
and the two quite different landscapes she'd seen,
Bluebell guardian showed her two long mirrors set
in the wall beside the window. 'Look at both
to show you *now* along with how you *used* to be
or *may* be in time, even the *best* way to be
beside what *seems* an answer to your dreams.'

In the left-hand glass she was more or less
the girl who'd wandered into the orchard at home,
though her eyes were sharp and bright with wonder,
she wore dazzling slippers, a rainbow-coloured
flower necklace and fine jewel-studded belt.
Behind her she could see as through a mist
all nine guardians holding out their gifts.

The other glass showed a tall young lady
in a gown made of moonbeams and lined
with silvery silk, slim patterned shoes to match,
the same flower necklace but worked in silver,
no Smith's belt but a girdle laced with
precious diamonds, pearls and opals. Beside her
lay a worn-out frock and threadbare sunhat.
Behind her in his moonlit armour stood
young Sir Cloudy who'd sprung from his horse,
plumed helmet doffed, waiting eagerly
for her to turn and greet him with a hand to kiss.

Turning away from the mirror she found all
the guardians in their rainbow-palace guise
waiting to greet her. And just as before
it was the tall figure clothed in white-rose-patterns
who spoke to her and once again offered a choice:
'What you choose, dearest Grace, decides the days
ahead and colours the long life you can expect.'
Views, mirrors, another test: so much she longed
to ask about, but White Rose was far from finished.

'Two pathways. The first like your journey
wound along with purpose, the other circled
round and round and back to where it started.
Two landscapes: one rich in colour and growth,
the other gleaming with full-moon mystery.
Two pictures: *now,* and as you might like to be
if you retrace your steps, meet Sir Cloudy, return to
his *Castle-in-the-Air* and live forever after
as his bride-to-be in moonlit make-believe.

Or you can live a life uncertain
as the travels you have completed
to make your gift of wonder come alive.
Wonder is not for wonderland. It keeps

hearts and minds open and ready to
accept much that cannot be explained away.
I'm sorry to say the knight's secret way
to the rainbow is only one he hopes to take
at the dark of the moon when no silver light
brings his world alive; but he never does.
He can't endure sunlight and falling rain
without which no colour-bow spans the sky.
He made a quest like yours, but moonlight captured him
as the carefree wood, under-hill halls
or rainbow garden might have enchanted you.

Guardians unfold like the living earth we tend,
working to make it loved. You live in time
and place and must decide how and where.'

How do you suppose Grace felt after hearing
all this? Once more so much turned out
to be quite different from what it seemed,
her dear friend Sir Cloudy just as lost
as Don when she found him blinkered and downcast.
Somehow in her heart she felt the wisdom of all
these words but she could not hope to piece
everything together at once, though she knew
the moon's fitful borrowed glimmer could never
replace daylight that embroiders the Earth,
as it was blessed with warmth, life and growth.
Uncle Edward used to talk about people
who did not want to change being in
a 'time-warp' and content to remain there.
'Must I decide now?' she asked White Rose.
'No: but try to think about your choices
as you descend the rainbow steps. A quiet time
before you meet those who wait to greet you.

You may think it's for the last time
but many will return in new guises.'
Then the speaker and all her companions returned
to their gazing and weaving. The far door opened
so Grace began her slow climb down countless
steps to where the bow bridge faded. Her back
foot left a flash of light on each crystal shelf,
but when she paused to look up the stairway
it was a fine mist of many colours.

XVIII

HOME?

We'll never know how Grace expected her travels to end, but she finds the truth in many hints she has been given that her adventures might well have been the beginning of many more.

When Grace was nearly at the rainbow foot
she could see several of her old friends waiting
but where was Sir Cloudy and his retinue
as she had viewed them from the palace window?
Where were the armed men on their proud horses,
bridles jingling, stamping and champing at the bit,
ready to escort her if she chose to go?
At least there would have been a ceremony,
time to bid her courteous host and friend farewell.

But then the words of White Rose came back to her:
if you retrace your steps and meet Sir Cloudy…
There were no steps back and now she noticed
her sturdy old shoes had somehow replaced
the gold-and-silver slippers Heartsease had provided
for the Shining Stairway. Below, and beyond
her friends, lay a narrow ravine, carved out
perhaps by the River of Day after rushing
tirelessly towards the Rainbow of rainbows.

When Grace was nearly at the rainbow foot she could see several of her old friends waiting…

Tracing the canyon line to where it bent away
she noticed a widespread, dark forest,
and near its edge could just pick out
a bevy of riders on white horses, their armour
glinting in sunlight, banners lowered and in haste
to reach the wood-edge as if it were a refuge.
All of which Grace took in very briefly,
none of it meaning much as she leapt
down the last few steps, eager to greet her friends:

familiar figures from her travels. Don the delver,
downcast no more, upright and proudly leaning on
his silver spade. This had helped him to wonder
about all the creatures that worked in the earth
without which there'd be no growth and colour.
He'd been Dame Nature's pupil and here she was
after guiding him along a rainbow journey
harder and darker than Grace's: a fine story
but even fuller of long short-cuts than hers!

Heartsease was there in her violet woodland cloak,
yellow-hooded. She'd brought a few uniformed
ladybird attendants and a small contingent
of green spear folk, restless and impatient
as if they'd no business to be standing idle.
Guardian Clover had sent some spring spirits
from the under-hill halls. Here they seemed
to be clothed in misty strands of rainbow pink
and ready to decorate this high, rocky place.

As they crowded round she thanked each one
or each group for their part in helping her
to complete travels filled with so many
surprising twists and turns, but she had more
to say to Don, whose needs had shaped her harder and darker
undertakings, though he didn't realise it.

'If you hadn't thought better of your doubts
at the edge of *The-Wood-That-Is-Not-There*
I wouldn't have visited Smith and learnt
to admire his craft or known the strange desert
wilderness and its wonderful Rock-Heart.
Nor would I have met Dame Nature
and found out how her helpers work for our world.'
Don replied: 'Thank you for not leaving me
in the lurch when you vanished into
the enchanted wood I could barely see,
and for making so many of your roundabout
adventures all part of starting me on mine.

I hear you've been closest to plants.
My travels have opened an ever-wider
and deeper world of insects, and wonder
has taught me how to understand the way they all
work together, whether or not they know it.
In the Rainbow Garden I was tempted to stay
for good-and-all with my own plot to work at
and creatures galore to study; but Dame Nature
persuaded me to move on and take my chance.'

It was time for Heartsease to speak to
both children about their way forward.
First Grace must think about what she'd glimpsed
from the last steps. 'Bright sun
glinted on the steel of armed riders retreating
fast into a dense forest. Sir Cloudy Lost-Heart
had ordered his followers back into
the wide, dark woodlands that form a border to
his palely-lit realms, a place to hunt by day
but secluded and safe from prying sunlight.
He had to brave open spaces to greet you.
Perhaps he lost his nerve and took flight.
Remember what White Rose told you.

Even if he'd followed Day-River gorge,
there's no way across to where we stand,
a gap that shows the distance between the way
you and he view the world. Your formal
farewells would have been waved from afar.

'This ever-deepening rift has other meanings
for you and Don. There are two ways back to
that daily life you've briefly left behind.
You can take a leap of faith over the edge,
trusting that all you've learnt will make Wonder
remove the stubborn blinkers that imprisoned you.
The drop feels as if someone has briefly opened
door on a windy day, and when it closes
you'll be back among familiar places and people.

You can be spirited across the chasm to where
your rainbow quest began, knowing it's enriched
the talent that drew the guardians to test you.
Now some warnings you don't have to heed.
Don: from the far cliff top you may return to
the dull moment when chance woke you within
a daydream to meet Grace. You might have to make
another start. And Grace, a leap may land you
in a far more testing place than your girlhood.

Hearing this both children were in no doubt
about which way home was best for them.
Unused to how he'd changed, Grace was surprised
when Don bowed respectfully to Heartsease and said:
'Thank you. I feel as if I want to
go on listening to your voice and guidance
but if it's best for me to take a leap back
and so be of more use to myself and others,
may I go at once and with my spade?'

'You've chosen well,' said Heartsease warmly.
'Your spade helped you along, and the quest for it
opened new avenues of wonder for Grace.
Hold it close but it must dissolve and return
as precious ore to Ancient Rock Heart's store.
Your gifts too, Grace, belong where they were received.
The jewel-studded belt will slip back to
Smith's cave, and that flower necklace to
locked vaults below *Castle-in-the-Air*.

'Wait here while I see Don safely home.'
She put an arm round the boy's shoulder
to guide him up the slope that hid the great crevice,
and as they left Grace noticed how
upright and confident Don looked,
so unlike that slouching, sulky lad she'd woken
near the gate into *The-Wood-That-Is-Not-There.*
It was the last she saw of him, and though
his story *may* be found, we can't trace it further.

When they had disappeared Graced turned
to talk to her other friends but they had vanished,
and the coarse grass among scattered rocks
showed no sign of anyone setting foot there.
As for this side of the rainbow bridge
it was like a striped waterfall hanging in
air, and there was no foothold in sight.
So she turned again to wait for Heartsease and watch
her bright hood top the heather-clad slope.

But she found herself looking at orchard trees
and beyond them a tall, thick hedge running beside
the long lane that skirted Aunt and Uncle's land.
Early summer sun shone brightly and made
everything glisten after a passing shower.
The geese she'd just fed forgot to quarrel,

preened themselves and flapped their idle wings.
Was it the rain or could she see more clearly?
Hawthorn leaves were a glossier dark green
than before, their pale berries ready to ripen
for winter-starved birds. Lichen-patterned bark
of the oldest pear tree made a silver-grey beard
finer than Woodmaster-Oak's trunk. At her feet
so many different grass-green families and armies
bustled into growth, and among them creeping
cheerfully back to flower, speedwells, camomile,
golden birds-foot trefoil and tufted ground ivy,
let wandering geese peck and trample where they would.

Along beside the hedge Grace was glad to see
foxgloves, stinking lords-and-ladies, meadowsweet
and whitening upturned umbrellas of parsley and hemlock.
On high in his elm tower a song thrush
repeated his warning: *my-castle...my-castle*!
Looking east beyond the house to where the shower
had passed she hoped to see a hint of rainbow.
Of course the sun was far too high to play upon
distant rain, but looking up she was amazed
to spot a most unusual many-coloured crest.
Have you ever seen a sun-shaft caught in
wispy cloud turn to watery stained-glass?
It's the closest you'll come to finding a rainbow flower.
Just then a familiar high-pitched, sweet voice
sang on the air just as she had heard it
in that very place only moments ago,
or so it now seemed, when her guide and guardian
had appeared in folds of airy, shimmering violet.

✣ Home? ✣

Among violets under hedge
farewell I wave to you.
Has Heartsease kept her pledge
lovingly to guide you?

Over ravine of River Day
I've brought you.
Time now to find your way
where dreams may lead you.

…she dragged the rickety gate open and closed in those ravaging geese, as uncle called them…

✣ Home? ✣

It made Grace wonder if 'dreams' could mean
being dreamy and lazy or moments and faces recalled
after waking. The dreams the Piper gave her always
seemed to lead to anxious times and hard choices.
As for being back home from somewhere else,
so much in this orchard reminded her
of places she was meant to have left behind.
Were all those wonders and adventures 'just
a dream'? Something she heard people say
about ideas, plans or fanciful hopes.

Still unable to believe no one had missed her
or might be searching orchard, lanes and fields beyond,
she dragged the rickety gate open and closed in
those ravaging geese, as uncle called them, skipped
across lawns to the ever-open back porch
and into the kitchen where cook's leftovers soup
simmered as invitingly as when she'd called for scraps.
How glad she was that nothing had changed.
So was she after all just the same Grace?

-♦-